Gone Missing

JEAN URE

Illustrated by Karen Donnelly

HarperCollins *Children's Books*

For Sarah Mason and Rachel Woolford

First published in Great Britain by HarperCollins *Children's Books* in 2007
HarperCollins *Children's Books* is a division of HarperCollins*Publishers* Ltd,
77-85 Fulham Palace Road, Hammersmith, London W6 8JB

The HarperCollins *Children's Books* website address is
www.harpercollinschildrensbooks.co.uk

1

Text © Jean Ure 2007
Illustrations © Karen Donnelly 2007

The author and illustrator assert the moral right to be
identified as the author and illustrator of this work.

ISBN-13   978 0 00 722459 3
ISBN-10   0 00 722459 1

Printed and bound in England by
Clays Ltd, St Ives plc

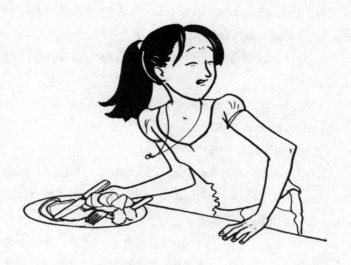

one

"*Eat.*"

"I won't!"

"You'll either do as you're told or you'll sit there for the rest of the day! Do I make myself clear?"

Crash. Bang. *Wallop.*

That's Dad, striking the table. This is me, shrieking at him: "I'd sooner starve!"

Whonk.

Me again, slamming the door as I rush from the room.

"Jade Rutherford, you come back here!"

Dad thunders after me, followed by Mum. (Kirsty just sits there, carrying on eating.)

"I will not have my meal times disrupted by tantrums!"

"Alec, leave her! It's not worth all this upset!"

Mum pleads, Dad bellows, I shriek.

"You can't force me!"

"Alec, *please.*" Now she's clutching at him. I wish she wouldn't! It's so degrading. "Let her be! She'll eat when she's hungry."

I yell that I *am* hungry. "But I'm not shovelling stinking, rotten flesh into myself! It's disgusting, it's unhygienic, it's repulsive!"

Dad bellows, again, that I will eat what I am given. "We don't have food fads in this house! We eat what the Lord has provided!"

I'm tempted to be smart and say that I thought it was Mum who'd provided. Instead I shriek, "Some weird kind of Lord, wanting us to eat dead stuff!"

I shouldn't have said it; I've gone too far. Dad's face turns slowly purple, like a big shiny aubergine. He shouts, "Right! That is enough! You get back in there and you sit yourself down and you *eat*."

He can't force me. Nobody can force me.

We stand there, facing each other, for what seems like minutes. Dad is breathing, very heavily.

"I'm warning you, my girl! You either eat what the rest of us eat, or you eat nothing."

"So I'll eat nothing! I'll get anorexic and I'll probably die. Then perhaps you'll be happy!"

Mum bleats, "Alec…"

"Veronica, you stay out of this!"

Dad stands firm. He's a great believer in standing firm. He will not be dictated to by a fourteen-year-old girl – especially not in his own house.

"If she feels that strongly," says Mum.

"She doesn't," snarls Dad. "It's all done to rile me!"

There may be a nugget of truth in what he says. Just a tiny little insy winsy nugget. At any rate, that's all I'm admitting to.

"Jade, please!" begs Mum. "Let's talk about this later. Come back, now, and eat your dinner."

"No way!" I turn, and gallop up the stairs three at a time. "He can take his lump of flesh and guzzle it himself!"

"*Jade!*"

"You'll have to put me in a straitjacket and use a feeding tube before you get it down me!"

"I wouldn't joke about it, if I were you!" bawls Dad. "It may yet come to that."

"In your dreams! I'd kill myself first."

Etc., etc. Day after day, same old thing. Dad bawling, me yelling, Mum humbling herself. Jade, *please*! Alec, *please*! And all to no avail, cos neither of us ever took the least bit of notice.

This is just one example of the rows that I used to have with my dad. Well, stepdad, actually, but Mum married him when I was only four, so you'd have thought by the time I was fourteen we'd have grown used to each other. It was OK when I was little. Fairly OK. He was always a whole lot stricter than anyone else's dad, but you accept that when you're a kid. You can't really do much else, it's just the way things are. It was when I got to be, like, twelve, thirteen, that the problems started. See, my dad is a very self-opinionated sort of person. Whatever he says is right, and if anyone says different then they are wrong, and that is all there is to it. No room for discussion. They are simply WRONG.

Unfortunately, I am somewhat that way inclined myself. Not that I automatically think everyone else is wrong, I like to believe that I have a reasonably open mind, but I do have these very strong opinions about all kinds of things. I think you have to have opinions, because, I mean, without them you are nothing but a mindless blob. The trouble is when your dad has one lot of opinions and you have another and they are just, like, at opposite ends of the spectrum, and neither of you will budge by so much as a centimetre.

Mum used to fall over backwards to keep Dad happy. *Ask your father. Listen to your father. Your father knows best.* Anything for a quiet life. My sister Kirsty, she's two years younger than me, she just used to keep her head down and say nothing. That way, she and Dad got on really well. She didn't cosy up to him, she wasn't that much of a creep, but if ever he said anything that I knew for a fact she disagreed with, cos like we'd discussed it together, she'd just go into silent mode. I guess it's one way of coping. It's just not my way! I think it's a bit dishonest, to tell you the truth. Like somebody once said, though I cannot now remember who, we all have to stand up and be counted.

Most of the rows I had with Dad tend to dissolve into a blur, there were so many of them. But I remember the one about the dead flesh cos I wrote it up in my journal. (Which I kept for almost a month, before the effort wore me out.) I was just so angry! Nobody, but *nobody*, should try to force someone to go against their principles, especially not your own dad. It's a form of bullying. He's the one with the power, and you're just there to do his bidding, no matter how evil. I was in such a rage! I didn't make a note of the actual date, but it was definitely a Sunday, cos that was the day we all sat down together for the ritual roast, and it was definitely during term time. The summer term, somewhere near the beginning, so it was still light outside and I

wasn't about to spend the rest of the evening skulking in my bedroom while he was fuming in the kitchen, stuffing himself with murdered pig, or whatever it was. I remember that I grabbed my jacket and whizzed back downstairs and out of the front door – closing it *really* quietly behind me – and went tearing up the road, with a great huffing and puffing, to Honey's place.

It was what I always did, when I felt the need to let off steam. Honey de Vito was my best, best, *very* best friend. Best of all time, ever. I know I will have other best friends during the course of my life, but I shan't ever be as close to one as I was with Honey.

I'm aware there were some people that thought it

odd, me and Honey being friends. There was a girl in my class, Marnie Wilkinson, who was, like, my *school* friend – Honey was my *out-of-school* friend – who actually asked me once what I saw in her.

She probably wasn't the only one who wondered this. It's so unfair, cos I don't expect anyone ever asked Honey what she saw in me. Honey was a bit of a loner at school. She was a couple of years older than me, so of course we were in different classes, and people from different classes never mix. It's just not done. Even if it were, me and Honey would never have hung out at school. I was one of those horrible loud, shrieking, show-off types. The sort that always gets invited to parties, always goes round in a gang, always manages to be the centre of attention. I suppose in a way I still am.

I'm still a bit loud and shrieky, and I am quite popular, but the fact is that I have never had a *real friend*. Not like Honey. Marnie was OK, we used to giggle together about boys and read magazines in the girls' toilets and swop clothes, and once I went to a sleepover at her place with a couple of others from our class. Everyone thought me and Marnie were bosom buddies, and I suppose on the surface I had far more in common with her than I did with Honey.

But me and Honey had been friends for such ages! Years and years. Ever since we were tiny babies in our prams, banging our little plastic rattles and beaming our toothless beams. Well, I'd have been toothless; Honey was a toddler. But she always simply *adored* babies. She used to trundle me round the garden in a wheelbarrow. Really sweet! Probably if we'd been brought up in a normal, civilised part of the country like other people we wouldn't ever have become friends. As it was,

Honey was practically the only person my age within a fifty-mile radius. Steeple Norton, where we were doomed to live out our excruciatingly boring existences, is just about the back of beyond. What you might call an *armpit*. Dead as a duck pond without any ducks. Out of school, me and Honey couldn't have been closer. We did everything together. We knew each other through and through. We never had to explain ourselves; we didn't have any secrets.

The thing is, people always had the wrong idea about Honey. If you'd asked anyone at school they'd have told you she was backward, and I know that's how she came across. She was sixteen, I was fourteen, and sometimes it was like she was even younger than Kirsty. But she wasn't *backward*. I mean, not like retarded, or anything. Just a bit immature. A bit… slow. And if you ask me that was mainly cos she was so unsure of herself. Cos she'd spent all her life being humiliated. Kirsty always said I kept up with her cos I could push her around, but that wasn't true, either. I was always nagging at her, for instance, to tell someone about her mum, about the way she treated her, but she never would. Where her mum was concerned, she wouldn't budge. I know that I was the one responsible for – well, for what happened. I know I was the one that talked her into it. But in the end she proved she had a mind of her own. Whatever people say, she wasn't just some sort of helpless glove puppet.

Anyway, that day, when Dad and I had our row about my eating habits, everything still lay in the future – though not so very far distant. Really, just a couple of weeks off. Not that I had any inkling of it, then; not for all my big talk. If someone had told me what I would set in motion, I wouldn't have believed them. Miss Harriman, our year group tutor when I was in Year 8, used to say that I was "rebellious by nature". She once warned me that if I wasn't careful I would come to a *sticky end*. So maybe Miss Harriman would have believed them. But not me! I'm one of those people, I have this very wild imagination. I tend to go off into realms of fantasy. *I'm gonna do this, I'm gonna do that. You just wait, you just see*. And then someone like Marnie will go, "Oh, yeah?" and I'll go, "Yeah!" and we'll both know that it's not really going to happen. Just a load of hot air, as my nan would say.

But being with Honey made me bold – and she was the one, when it came to the crunch, who said go for it.

It was her mum who opened the door to me when I went storming round, that Sunday afternoon. She said, "Oh, hallo, Jade!" with one of her big, bright, sugary smiles, showing all her lipsticky teeth and breathing booze over me.

I said, "Hallo, Mrs de Vito," but I didn't smile back. Not a proper smile. I didn't trust Honey's mum. She was always sweet as pie to me and mean as maggots to Honey. She treated Honey like dirt, and especially when she'd been "at the bottle", as they say.

I once remarked to Mum that I thought Mrs de Vito drank too much, and Mum said, "Poor soul! She's had enough to make her." She meant because of Mr de Vito going and walking out on her, leaving her to cope as a single mum. But not all single mums get drunk and are horrid to their daughters. I hated Honey's mum for the way she put Honey down all the time.

I asked her if Honey was there and she gave this little laugh, like she was really amused by the question. She said, "Why wouldn't she be? She never sets foot outside the house unless it's with you. Go on, you can go up." And then, as I headed for the stairs, "It's beyond me what she does up there."

I could have told her what Honey did: she hid from her mum. Or at any rate, did her best to keep out of harm's way. Out of *tongue's* way. She really only came down when she had to, like at mealtimes – when there were any mealtimes, which mostly there weren't. Mostly Honey just took something out of the fridge, or opened a tin.

"*Hunneee!*" I banged on the door of her room. "It's Jade, let me in!"

Sometimes she kept her door locked. She'd get home from school and help herself to some food, take it upstairs with her and stay there right round till morning. When she did this, it usually meant her mum had been drinking. The door was locked that afternoon.

"Hey!" I rattled at the handle. "Let me in, I want to talk!"

"Sorry." She opened the door a crack and pulled me through. "I didn't hear you."

"I've been practically battering the place down!"

Apologetically she said she had been listening to music; this group called the Beany Boys, that she really loved. She used to lie on the bed, with her headphones on, and the volume turned way up. She could stay like that for hours. I'd even rung two or three times in ne evening and got no reply, even though I knew she was there.

"Honestly, I am *seething*," I said. I had to talk, or I would burst!

"You've had another row with your dad," said Honey.

"Yes, I have!" I hurled myself on to the bed. "He's driving me nuts! I can't take much more of it."

"What's he done now?"

It was all the invitation I needed. I was off! Railing on about Dad being a control freak and a bully. A sadist. A monster.

"Always forcing me to do what *he* thinks is right. Never mind what *I* think. I'm old enough to make up my own mind! It's a matter of principle. Like when I told him I didn't want to go to his stupid church any more? He practically wanted to burn me at the stake!"

"Yes, I remember," said Honey.

"Like something out of the Dark Ages! Like accusing people of being witches."

Dad hadn't talked to me for weeks after I'd dug in my heels and said I wasn't going to church any more. It's one of the things he is most fanatical about; I suppose you might almost call him a religious maniac. Well, compared with normal, balanced people. He's what's known as an Elder in the Family of God, which is like really really strict and totally against anything which might come under the heading of *fun*. Mum's a Family member, too, and so is Kirsty. I used to be, until I rebelled. It just got, like, too much. Every week, the same old thing. Trundling off in the car, miles and miles, for Sunday gathering. Gathering goes on for hours! And everyone so terribly *holy*.

I told him, "you don't have to go to church to be a good person. You don't even have to believe in *God* to be a good person!"

Dad was just *so* self-opinionated.

"Now it's meat," I said. "Just because he eats it, everyone else has to. And if you don't, then – God, I'm starving!" I reached out a hand and helped myself from a plate of goodies on the bedside table. "If you don't, then it's like some kind of blasphemy. He'd sooner let me *die* than eat what I want. I told him, he'll have to put me in a straitjacket before he gets dead muck down my throat! He actually threatened me. He actually—"

"Excuse me," said Honey, "but did you know you're eating sausage rolls?"

"No, I didn't, why didn't you *tell* me?" I shrieked.

"I just did," said Honey.

"But I've swallowed them!"

"Gosh."

Honey regarded me, very solemnly. I think she may have been laughing at me, just a little bit. Just because I was the bossy one and she was the meek one, it didn't mean she was in awe of me, or anything. It's what people didn't realise. They only saw her as someone slow, and awkward, and a bit babyish, cos that's how she came across in situations where she wasn't sure of herself. But when it was just the two of us, when she felt safe, she could give as good as she got. I wouldn't have wanted a friend that was all creepy crawly.

I was still mouthing on – all about Dad, and how I couldn't put up with much more of it, I would have to get out, I would have to leave home, it was becoming unbearable – when Honey leaned forward to take the sausage rolls away from me and I saw this huge red blister on her arm.

"God," I cried, "where did that come from?"

Her face immediately turned as red as the blister. She had this very pale skin, and she used to blush very easily.

"I burned myself."

"How?"

She hung her head. "On a saucepan."

I didn't ask her how it happened, but I could guess. Honey was always doing things to herself – tripping over, stubbing her toe, spraining ankles, breaking wrists. She was quite an uncoordinated sort of person, like at school no one ever wanted her on their team because they knew she would mess things up. But she was a thousand times worse when she was around her mum. Her mum used to nag at her all the time. Nag at her, sneer at her, even poke fun at her. It got Honey so nervous, she just used to go to pieces. That was when the accidents occurred.

"You know what?" I said.

"What?"

"We both ought to get out. Not just me! Both of us."

Honey hooked her hair back over her ears. I

remember her eyes went all big and apprehensive. "You mean—"

"Leave home!"

"Like… *run away*?"

"Yes. Absolutely! Why not?"

Honey whispered: "You're not serious?"

I told her that I was in deadly earnest. I really meant it! This wasn't just one of my fantasies.

two

"But where would we go?"

It was the day following my big row with Dad. My *latest* big row with Dad. Me and Honey were on our way back from school. We were the ones that lived furthest away, so it was just the two of us left on the bus. Kirsty had stayed on for something: the drama club or whatever. Not for a detention! Little Goody Two-Shoes never got detention. I was the one that got those.

"I mean…" Honey lowered her voice to a whisper. "*Where?*"

"We could always go and stay with Darcy," I said.

I'd been fantasising like mad all night. I'd got it all worked out – well, the broad details. "All we'd have to do is just get ourselves down to London, then jump on a tube train. I know how to do it! I've been down to London, I've been on a tube. 'S easy! They've got maps and everything."

Honey gazed at me, doubtfully. She had her lower lip all bunched up and was gnawing at it like a rabbit.

"Stop doing that," I said. "It makes you look daft!" Honey was really pretty, far prettier than me, but she had this kind of vacant expression she sometimes put on, like her brain had gone to mush.

"*Concentrate*," I said.

"Sorry." Honey stopped gnawing her lip and sat up, very straight and stiff and purposeful. "OK," she said. "I'm concentrating."

"We get the train to London, right?"

She nodded. She still seemed doubtful.

"We get on a tube, we go to Darcy's place. Yes?"

"Y-yes. I— I s'ppose."

"Now what's the matter? Darcy said, if ever I wanted a place to crash— "

"She meant you," said Honey. "Not me."

"Both of us!"

"No, *you*."

27

It was true that Darcy had been my friend rather than Honey's. She'd always said that Honey was "soft in the head". I used to tell her it wasn't true, but maybe, looking back on it, I didn't stick up for Honey quite as much as I should have done. I'm not easy to impress, I really am not, but I think I was sort of, like, a bit *smitten* where Darcy was concerned. I mean, this was a truly wild and whacky person! I'd never met anyone quite like her. We hung out together all through Year 8 and part of Year 9. We were thick as thieves! Sometimes we *were* thieves... Darcy used to nick things off the supermarket shelves, and I used to copy her. Only small things, but it was just so exciting, I used to get prickly all over. It was like being in the SAS, or something. Going off on these dangerous missions.

Yeah, well, OK, I can see now that it was wrong. I knew at the time that it was wrong. But we never took anything valuable. We just did it for kicks.

Once when her mum had gone off somewhere she stayed at my place for a couple of days, though I have to say that was a complete disaster owing to Dad and his insane prejudices. He took one look and that was it: *that girl has got to go*. She couldn't actually go cos she didn't have anywhere to go to and not even Dad would throw someone out on the street, but afterwards he said

she was a bad influence and I hadn't got to see her any more. We had some of our *worst* rows over that. Not that it stopped me seeing her! It hardly could, considering we went to the same school. Course, when Darcy got excluded Dad was like "I told you so! I said that girl was no good." That was when Darcy's mum said she couldn't cope and sent her off to London to live with her sister, and I took up with Marnie, instead.

"Darcy didn't like me," said Honey.

"She didn't even know you!" I said.

"She wouldn't want me."

"Look, we'd only be there a few days, till we found somewhere else. I'm not going without you," I said. "How could I go off and leave you here, all by yourself? If we do this, we gotta do it together!"

She was back at her lip munching again. I did wish she wouldn't!

"*Honey?*" I said. "Are you listening?"

She dipped her head.

"So are we agreed? We could go and crash with Darcy. Just for a few days, till we get sorted. OK?"

The bus pulled up at the Green Man, and we both got out. I said, "*Yes?*"

"Yes, all right," said Honey. "But what would we do afterwards?"

"After we got sorted?"

"After we'd stopped crashing with Darcy."

"We'd go and crash somewhere else!"

"But where?"

"How do I know where?" My fantasies hadn't reached that far. I'd only got as far as the actual running away. "I can't plan everything at once," I said. "Some things you just have to… wait for them to happen!"

*****

"What we have to do," I said, "we have to cover our tracks."

It was Tuesday, and we were on the bus again. Going in to school, this time.

"It's very important," I said. "We have to lay a trail."

Honey had been looking faintly worried, like she didn't quite know what I was talking about. When I said *lay a trail*, she brightened.

"Bread crumbs!" she said.

I said, "Yeah, right! Bread crumbs! Remember those two boys we met that time? Ian, and—" I waved a hand.

"Duncan." She blushed. Duncan had been the one she fancied. I think he'd fancied her a bit, too. We'd gone into Birmingham for the day, just me and Honey on our own, and we'd bumped into these two lads in McDonald's and got talking. We'd really hit it off! Well, to be honest, Honey and Duncan had hit it off. Boys always went for Honey. In spite of her dad being Italian, she had this silvery hair and ivory skin, like her mum, but with her dad's eyes, deep and dark, like rich chocolate. I guess she was what you'd call striking. Mum always said that with looks like those she would need to be careful. I knew what she meant. It doesn't do to be too trusting, and Honey had this tendency, she'd trust anyone that was nice to her.

"Duncan McAleer," said Honey.

Wow! She'd even remembered his surname. It was more than I'd done. I hadn't even remembered his *first* name. All I remembered was that they'd lived in Glasgow. They'd given us their addresses and said to call if ever we were up there.

I'd chucked the addresses in the bin cos a) I couldn't see I'd ever be going to Glasgow, not in the foreseeable future, and b) even if I did I wouldn't particularly want to meet up with them again. Duncan wasn't actually too bad, but Ian had been a geeky little thing with red hair and a pointy nose and a face like a ferret. Yuck! Not my type at all.

"Is that where we're going to go?" said Honey. "To Glasgow?"

I said, "No! That's where the *bread crumbs* are going to go." I could see that I'd lost her, but the bus was starting to fill up and I didn't have time to explain. "I'll tell you about it later."

"Why can't you tell me now?"

"Because it's a secret," I hissed. "*Our* secret… just between you and me. Right?"

She nodded. "OK."

"Promise you won't tell anyone!"

Honey was always very biddable. She ran a finger across her throat. "Slit my throat and hope to die."

I giggled. "You probably would die, if you slit your throat!"

She meant "cross my heart" but she sometimes got things a bit muddled. It could be quite funny.

On the way home that afternoon, I explained to her what I meant about the bread crumbs. I'd stayed awake half the night hatching elaborate plots, laying false trails, like I was in some kind of spy movie.

"We have to make them think we've gone to Glasgow. Not London. We don't want them to be on to us!"

Honey muched at her lip. "Why can't we do it the other way round? Make them think we've gone to London?"

"Because we *are* going to London!"

"I'd rather go to Glasgow."

"We don't know anyone in Glasgow!"

"Yes, we do. We know Duncan! I'd rather go and stay with Duncan than with Darcy."

"Well, we can't, cos I've lost his address. And anyway, we don't actually *know* him."

"I don't actually know Darcy."

"No, well I do, and that's where we're going."

Honey fell quiet for a bit. I could see she was turning things over in her mind.

"Are we *really* going to run away?" she said.

"We are if things don't improve at home! You don't know what it's like, living with my dad. And you can't go on living with your mum. She'll destroy you! You know that, don't you? You do know?"

I fixed her with this stern look. Honey just made a vague mumbling sound and let her eyes slide away. Honey's mum was like a forbidden subject; she wouldn't ever talk about her. I went on about Dad practically non stop, but Honey never once said anything bad about her mum. I knew she was a bit frightened of her – not physically, I don't mean, cos I don't think her mum was ever violent. It might almost have been better if she had been; at least then someone would have had to sit up and take notice. As it was, I think I was probably the only person that knew how hateful she could be to Honey. Honey was just scared, the whole time, of displeasing her. Doing the wrong thing. Saying the wrong thing. Dropping something, breaking something. Being told she was stupid.

Stupid, useless, hopeless. Clumsy, gawky. Nothing but a liability, can't ever do anything right. Totally moronic! Drive me up the wall.

These were all things I'd heard Mrs de Vito say to Honey. When she'd had too much to drink she actually used to jeer at her. Make fun of her.

"Look at it! Great lumping thing! Can't even walk straight."

And then she'd imitate Honey moving across the room, bumping into chairs and knocking stuff over. "What's the matter with you? You got cerebral palsy, or something?"

She could be really nasty. Sometimes she used to try and rope me in. She'd look at me and roll her eyes, like she was expecting me to agree with her. I hated it when she did that! It made me feel so bad for Honey. I mean, they were cruel, the things she said. She didn't deserve Honey being so loyal! Maybe, in spite of everything, Honey still loved her; I guess it's always possible. I just don't know. But I honestly did feel she had to get away, I really did! I wasn't only thinking of me. At least, I don't think I was.

That evening, I sat upstairs in my bedroom laying trails of bread crumbs... all the way to Glasgow! First off, I doodled hearts and flowers all over my school books, with the name DUNCAN in big capitals. (I chose Duncan rather than ferret face. I couldn't stand the thought of being linked with ferret face!) Then I took our surnames, McAleer and Rutherford, and crossed out all the letters we had in common. Precisely two! I'd have been in despair if he'd really been my boyfriend.

I got a bit carried away with the doodling. I was still at it when Mum and Dad got home from the shop (the Steeple Norton Mini Mart. Oh, please!) and I had to go downstairs and report on school and whether I'd done my homework. It was like the Spanish Inquisition every

night. Dad used to say, "This doesn't please me any more than it pleases you." He never did it with Kirsty because Kirsty could be trusted. She'd never bunked off school or failed to hand in her homework three weeks running. But all that had been back in the winter term! Back when I was still mates with Darcy. It was very belittling that Dad still kept grilling me.

I told him that I was *doing* my homework. Dad said, "You'd better be." I said, "I *am*!" and went rushing back upstairs to scatter more bread crumbs. I would look up train times! On the computer, Birmingham to Glasgow. I knew the first thing the police would do when they started to investigate would be to take away the computer and examine it. They can find out all sorts of things, from a computer. Just to make sure, I even went to Google and put in the word "Glasgow", so they'd think I'd been looking at the map. I'd have liked to put in Stonebridge Park, which was where Darcy had gone to live with her sister. I knew that Stonebridge Park was in London, and I knew you could get there on a tube train, cos Darcy had told me. She had said it was totally brilliant.

"You can be in the West End in thirty minutes!"

I wasn't bothered about trains from Birmingham; I knew there were plenty of those, all times of the day. Money was the real problem. I had some saved up in a piggy bank – an old china pig with a slit in its back, which had belonged to one of my nans when she was a girl – and I thought I probably had enough for a single fare to London, but it wasn't going to leave very much over. What did other kids do when they ran away? Did they steal off their parents? I couldn't steal off mine, or only very tiny amounts. Dad didn't believe in having large sums of money lying around. He'd been robbed twice at the shop and it had made him very grim. But I didn't think most people would exactly have fortunes waiting to be taken, so what did kids do? I had a sneaking suspicion that maybe they went on the streets and begged, or even worse, they sold themselves. I wouldn't want to do that! No way!

I decided not to think about it. As I'd said to Honey, you can't plan *everything* in advance. Sometimes, you just have to wait and see what happens.

That's the good thing about fantasies. If there's a part you can't work out, you just skate over it and move on to the next bit.

It *was* still a fantasy. But growing more and more real, every day.

*****

Next morning, at school, Marnie comes up to me and says, "Hey! Wanna know something?" So I'm like, "Yeah, what?" She tells me that this boy, Rory Mansell, that's in Year 10, has a thing about me. She knows this cos she's going out with Jason Dobbs that's also in Year 10. She says Rory told Jason in the hope that he would tell Marnie and Marnie would tell me, and then maybe I would—

Would what? Marnie giggles and says, "Ask him if he'd like to go on a date?"

I think to myself that if Rory Mansell wants to go on a date he could ask me himself, but Marnie says he's too shy. I say in that case he's a wimp.

"He's not a wimp," says Marnie, "he's just scared you'll turn him down." Then she tells me off for being prejudiced and says, "He's actually quite nice."

He's not bad, I agree, but as I explain to Marnie, I don't really fancy him. Marnie says, "So who do you fancy? You haven't been out with anyone for ages! You'll get out of the habit if you're not careful. People'll start thinking you're a lesbian!"

I say, "Now who's being prejudiced?" And then, without any warning, I hear myself blurt out, "There is someone I fancy!"

"Oh?" Marnie spins round. All ears. "Who's that, then?"

"This boy I met. In Birmingham. Me and Honey, we bumped into them, there were two of them, they were down here from Glagow and we all got talking and—"

My voice burbles on. It's got a will of its own. I can't control it, it's gone mad! Now it's telling Marnie how me and this boy have been speaking on the phone every week. We've been texting, we've been emailing.

We fancy each other *like crazy*.

Marnie says, "Wow! What's his name? How old is he? Gimme, gimme, I want to know!"

I say that I can't give her his name. "It's a secret!"

Marnie says, "Why? Is he someone famous?"

I struggle with a momentary temptation to say yes, but manage to resist it. I say no, he's not famous, he's just an ordinary boy.

"So why's it a secret?"

"Cos *he's* a secret! I shouldn't ever have mentioned him. I don't want Dad finding out! You know what my dad's like. He nearly went ballistic that time I went out with Soper. He *did* go ballistic!"

Marnie says, "Yeah, well… Soper." She then agrees with me, however, that my dad is impossible. "I'm surprised he even lets you have a mobile phone."

I say, "He wouldn't, if he had his way. It's only cos of Mum."

"I bet he checks on your calls!"

I mutter darkly that nothing would surprise me. "It's like living under a dictator."

"So what you gonna do?" says Marnie. "About this boy?"

I tell her that I don't yet know. "But if things get much worse, with my dad—"

"What? What?" She's all breathless and eager. "What d'you reckon you'll do?"

I say, "Something desperate!"

I spend the rest of the day trying to decide whether I've finally flipped and started to believe my own fantasies, or whether I've just been laying more bread crumbs. I decide that it's got to be bread crumbs. It's part of the trail! If Honey and me do run away – *when* Honey and me run away – the police will be bound to talk to Marnie. She'll be one of the first they talk to. And she'll just be bursting to tell them about "this boy she met that lives in Glasgow". I begin to feel rather pleased with myself. I'm obviously good at this sort of thing!

I do a bit of thinking about Rory, wondering whether he's really a wimp or just that mythical creature, a boy that's sensitive. But no, that's *truly* sexist. I'm sure there are boys that are sensitive, they just don't like to show it. Soper wasn't, of course. He'd have bashed someone's head in, if they'd suggested he was sensitive.

I think for a while about Soper. I try to remember what his first name was, but I can't. He was always just *Soper*; he was that sort of boy. The sort of boy that Dad thought should be locked up and the key thrown away. I know he was a bit mad and bad, but it was just totally *humiliating* when Dad actually chucked him out of the house. It was like, "Never darken my door again". We had the hugest row of all time over Soper.

That was when I finally rebelled and said I wasn't going to his stupid church any more. I did it to pay Dad out! I knew if there was one thing that would really upset him above all else, it would be having to admit that he'd lost control. That *one of his daughters* was leaving the Family. That was like heresy! That was like denying God.

The church thing had happened just a month ago; things had been getting steadily worse ever since. Dad was cold and tight-lipped, I was defiant. Sometimes I thought he hated me. Sometimes I thought I hated him.

He was convinced I did things for no reason than to annoy him, and I have to admit that he was partly right. But I had to assert myself! I mean, otherwise I would just have been ground down.

Later that day I gaze at Rory across the assembly hall. He catches me at it, and blushes. I think to myself that Dad would probably approve of Rory – well, as much as he'd approve of any boy. But even if he did, we'd still fall out. Dad and I are fated to disagree about pretty well everything. In any case, he's not my sort. Rory, I mean. He's too nice! How could I go out with a boy that Dad  approved of??? It's not worth staying on to be oppressed and humiliated just for the sake of going out with any stray male that happens to be available. I have more pride than that!

On the other hand, as Marnie reminded me, I haven't been out with a boy for simply months. That's not normal! Leave it too long and people will think I'm not interested. Plus I shall forget how to do it. How to talk to them. How to *be* with them. Cos being with a boy is definitely not the same as being with a girl.

It's Dad's fault. It's all Dad's fault! How can I ever hope to grow up sane and well balanced with him thwarting me at every turn? I feel in such a muddle!

When Honey asks me, on the way home, whether we are still going to *do it* – "That thing that you were talking about?" – I tell her yes, I'm working on it. Honey says, "So when do you think it will be?"

What does she expect me to say? It's not something you can put in your diary, like a dentist appointment. I tell her that I'm waiting to see what happens. "I'm giving him *one more chance*."

"Oh." Honey nods. "All right."

I say, "Why? You didn't want to go right now, did you?"

"I just thought you'd decided."

"I haven't decided anything! Have you?"

"No. I thought you had."

I tell her that I haven't made up my mind. *Yet.* "But if he comes on heavy just one more time—"

"That'll be it?" says Honey.

I say that that will definitely be it. "Cos I have had *enough*!"

three

Sunday was looming, with its roast and two veg. Dad insists on his roast and two veg, even in the height of summer. He sits there, sweating, and forcing himself to eat, like it's some kind of holy ritual. Like God has spoken to him. "And on Sunday, thou shalt consume flesh." Just so long as he didn't expect *me* to consume it. Dad, I mean, cos I don't believe in God. At least, I don't think I do.

I really didn't like having rows with Dad. I didn't go out of my way to have them, which Mum seemed to think I did; they just happened. I wasn't looking forward to another meat argument. I knew it would end in Dad banging on the table and me shrieking, the same as it had last Sunday, but I was determined to stand my ground.

Sunday morning, when she came back from Gathering, Mum called me into the kitchen. I thought she was going to warn me not to make a fuss, just eat what everyone else was eating in order to keep Dad happy. Mum would do almost anything to keep Dad happy. I was all prepared to put up a fight when she kind of took the wind out of my sails by saying, "Your father and I have been talking. He is still waiting for you to repent, but there is obviously no point in forcing you. It has to come from the heart. In the meantime you must make your peace with the Lord as best you may. I just pray he forgives you."

I said, "Forgives me for what?"

"Rejecting his bounty. It is not up to us to reject what the Lord has seen fit to provide."

Whew! Mum doesn't usually talk like this; she is usually quite normal. I guessed they'd been discussing me at Gathering. It was probably Dad who'd written the script for her.

I said, "Does that mean you're not going to nag me to eat dead stuff any more?"

Mum suddenly switched back to being Mum. "Not as long as you promise to eat everything else. I don't want you getting anorexic."

I assured her that I would glut on vegetable matter as much as she liked. I have no objections to potatoes and cauliflower. I said this to Mum. "Vegetables aren't pumped full of antibiotics – plus they don't have their throats cut."

Kirsty, who was laying the table, at once said, "No, they just get pulled up by the roots! How'd you like to be pulled up by the roots? Vegetables have feelings too, you know."

"Girls, please don't start," said Mum. "We don't need any smart mouth. Just remember, your dad's been working hard all week, he deserves a bit of peace and quiet on his day of rest."

Dad may have agreed there wasn't any point in forcing me, but he obviously wasn't pleased about it. He was in a foul mood from the word go. You could always tell when Dad was in a mood. He'd be ominously quiet, and his cheeks would turn a purply pink and his lips purse into this thin line. I guess what it was, he resented me being allowed to get away with something. Cos that's how he would have seen it. He'd have gone to Gathering all stiff and self-righteous, thinking everyone would be on his side and say how he'd got to tie me to a table leg and force-feed me, or lock me in my room and starve me into submission. He'd have liked to do that. He'd have felt he was carrying out God's mission. As it was, he sat and simmered all through lunch, seething as he watched me eat my vegetables. When he finally blew, it was like Vesuvius erupting. And over something utterly *trivial*.

Me and Kirsty had been talking about this teacher at school, Mrs Sebag. A stupid name, if ever there was one! I said, "She ought to be called *Old*-Bag, the way everything sags."

Kirsty giggled.

"That's not very nice," said Mum.

"She's not a very nice woman," said Kirsty. You can bet if little Miss Goody Two-Shoes says someone's not very nice, they're positively disgusting. "She's squalid,"

said Kirsty. It was our latest term of abuse. "She's squalid and she's *vicious*."

I said, "Yes, and she has a face like a bottom."

Kirsty giggled again.

"Great big fat cheeks like bum cheeks, and—"

It was then that Dad exploded.

"I will not tolerate that sort of talk on the Lord's day!" BANG. THUD. "How *dare* you speak of one of your teachers in those terms? It's about time you learned some respect!" CRASH. WALLOP. He was pounding the table so hard, all the cutlery was bouncing. Even Kirsty was looking a bit alarmed.

Mum said, "Alec—"
But Dad was on his feet
and bellowing.

"*Are you listening to
me?*" He planted both

fists on the table and leaned across, to glare into my face. His eyes were all bloodshot. "I have had just about enough of your boorish behaviour! What is it with you? Do you set out on purpose to upset us all? Does it give you some kind of perverted pleasure? Do you really think your mother and your sister want to sit here and listen to that kind of language?"

I said, "What are you on about? I didn't use four-letter words!"

Mum wailed, "Jade, please, stop it!"

"I won't stop it, he's mad! What's wrong with bum cheeks? Everybody's got some! We were made that way... *the Lord* made us that way. Blame Him if you don't like it! Not me. I didn't give us bum cheeks!"

I really thought for a minute that Dad was going to hit me. Not that he ever had, but there is always a first time. He stood there, with his fists on the table, breathing heavily and this vein throbbing in his forehead. I did my best to stare him out, but the honest truth is that I was actually a bit frightened. My dad is a big man; he could do a lot of damage. It really isn't sensible to provoke him. Not when he's in one of his rages.

Mum said again, "Alec!" She tugged nervously at his sleeve, but he elbowed her off.

I pushed my chair back. Dad snarled, "Who gave you permission to leave the table?"

"I've finished," I said.

"You've finished when I say you've finished! Sit down and clear your plate."

Mutinously, I did so, shovelling the last few scrapings of pudding into my mouth. "*Now* can I go?"

"You can go up to your room."

I said, "I don't want to go up to my room! I'm going round to Honey's."

I made for the door, but Dad's voice came bellowing after me.

"You're doing no such thing! You go up to your room and you stay there until I tell you it's time to come out!"

I looked from him to Mum. I couldn't believe this! I said, "Mum?"

Quietly she said, "Just do as your father tells you."

"But I—"

"*Do it!*" Dad was across the room and flinging open the door. He pointed, dramatically, up the stairs. "*Go to your room!*"

I shouted, "This is like living in some kind of soap opera!" but I didn't really have much choice. Not with Dad in that sort of mood.

I tore up the stairs and into my bedroom, slamming the door behind me. My heart was hammering. He couldn't treat me like this! I wasn't a child, I was fourteen years old. He couldn't keep me shut up against my will!

I sank down on to the bed. My limbs had gone all trembly, and my heart was still racing. Vengeful thoughts went spurting through my head. I snatched up the phone and punched out Honey's number. Let her answer! Let her answer! *Please*.

"Hallo?"

"Honey?" I said. "It's happened."

 There was a silence, then Honey said, "You mean—"

"We're going! I've had enough!"

More silence.

"Honey? Did you hear me? This is it, he's blown it. We're getting out!"

"Yes, all right," said

Honey. "If that's what you think we ought to do."

"It is!"

"So do you want me to get ready?"

I was surprised how calm she was. This was some big step we were taking! I'd have expected her to at least um and ah a bit. Instead, all she could say was "Do you want me to get ready?"

I told her to wait till I gave the OK. I had visions of her mum walking in to find Honey shoving clothes into her rucksack.

"Leave it till the last minute. I'll tell you when."

"So we're not going straight away?"

"We can't go *straight away*," I said.

"So when are we going?"

"Mm… I dunno! Soon. This week, maybe. We'll go this week! Cos it's half term, right?"

Honey said, "R-right." She was starting to sound a bit doubtful.

"We're definitely going," I said. "Sit and think what you want to take with you. Not your whole wardrobe, we can't carry loads of stuff. Just what'll go in your rucksack. Yeah?"

"Yeah."

"OK?"

"We are definitely going?"

"Yes, I told you! In the week."

Monday, maybe. Or maybe Wednesday, or Thursday. That would give me more time to plan. I needed to plan! I put the phone down and sat on the edge of my bed to do

what I had told Honey to do, think what I wanted to take with me. I *had* to go. I had to get out. I couldn't stand another minute of it! Dad had to be taught that he couldn't get away with treating me like that. He'd be sorry when I'd gone! When he had to confess, at Gathering, that his daughter had run away. Driven from home by his beastly bullying.

The phone rang and I snatched it up. I thought it might be Marnie, but it was Honey. She was all breathless and tense. She said, "If we're going to go, I think we should go now."

I said, "Why, what—"

"*Now!*" said Honey.

"You mean, like, right this minute?"

"*Now!*"

I said, "Why?"

"Cos I think now would be a good time."

"But *why*? I mean—"

"Let's just *do* it!" said Honey.

She talked me into it. Left to myself, I don't really think I ever would have gone. Not really. Not for all my plotting and planning. But there was an urgency in Honey's voice, and I couldn't lose face. I mean, I was the one that had been pushing for it.

So I made a snap decision. Sometimes you have to. "OK! Get ready. I'll be round as soon as I can, I've just got to wait for them to go out. Oh, and see if you can grab any money. As much as you can!"

I put the phone down, and this tingle of anticipation

went zinging through me. We were doing it! We were actually doing it! I yanked my rucksack off the top of the wardrobe and began frantically stuffing things into it. I'd already been over in my mind what I'd take with me. Just basics. And money! I pulled out the rubber bung in the belly of my piggy bank and a flood of coins cascaded over the duvet. I'd just about clawed up the last 2p when there was a tap at the door and Mum's voice said, "Jade?" Hastily, I kicked my rucksack out of sight, beneath the bed.

"Yes?" I stretched myself out, on top of the duvet. Mum came in, looking a bit flustered.

"We're just about to go… are you sure you don't want to come with us? Auntie Claire would be so pleased!"

"I thought I was being held prisoner?" I said.

"Oh, Jade!" Mum sat down, beseechingly, on the bed. "I wish you'd come and apologise to your dad! Just tell him you're sorry and you won't do it again. It would mean so much to him! He does love you, you know."

I grunted. "He's got a funny way of showing it."

"It's not easy for him. You know what Nana Rutherford's like."

Yeah, yeah! That was always the excuse: Dad's mum was sour and crotchety. She hadn't cuddled him when he was a baby. So now we all had to suffer.

"Jade! Please." Mum took my hands between hers. When Dad wasn't there to loom over her, Mum was quite a touchy-feely kind of person. Me and Kirsty had had loads of cuddles, on the quiet. That is, when Dad wasn't around to cast gloom and despair. Sometimes I used to feel sorry for Mum, being married to such a tyrant. Other times I just felt cross and resentful.

Right at this moment, I wasn't quite sure how I felt. Irritated, cos of Mum using emotional blackmail, mixed with guilt at what I was planning to do.

"He works so hard," said Mum. "His family means everything to him! He doesn't enjoy telling you off, it's just... well! He's under a lot of pressure, and he worries about you."

I muttered that I didn't know what he had to be worried about, but I let myself be persuaded. For Mum's sake, really. I am such a soft touch! I went back downstairs with her and found Dad backing the car out, and I took a deep breath and I told him that I was sorry. Even then, I could still have rung Honey and said I'd changed my mind. I might have, too. If Dad had just come half way to meet me! But he didn't. His face remained set like a stone. Coldly he said, "Don't you dare to talk to me like that again." And that was that.

I went back indoors. Kirsty said, "Oh, you broke out!" I told her to shut up. Mum looked at me, hopefully.

"So are you going to come with us?"

I shook my head.

"Oh, Jade, do! Auntie Claire will be so disappointed."

I snarled, "*No!*" and tore back upstairs. I waited till

they had all gone off, till the car was out of sight, then I pulled my rucksack from under the bed and headed for the door.

And that was when it struck me: it was Sunday! There aren't any buses on a Sunday. *Damn.* Damn, damn, damn! Even when you tried to run away from this horrible armpit of a place, you couldn't do it.

I refused to be beaten. My mind was made up! One way or another, we were definitely going.

I marched downstairs and into the garage, where the bikes were kept. Dad had had this idea, when we were younger, that we should all keep fit by cycling. We used to go on these mad family outings, round the

countryside, until one memorable day Dad got into a slanging match with a lorry driver and after that we didn't do it any more.

Determinedly, I wheeled a couple of bikes out of the garage and set off up the road to collect Honey. She must have been waiting just inside the front door cos she shot out immediately. The big beam on her face faded when she saw the bikes.

"What are they for?"

"It's Sunday," I said. "*No buses.* Remember?"

"Oh." Her mouth dropped open.

"Don't do that," I said, "it makes you look daft. Here!"

I pushed one of the bikes at her. She backed away, as if it were some kind of wild animal.

"We can't cycle all the way to Birmingham!"

You had to be very patient with Honey. It was no good getting mad at her, it just slowed her up even more.

"We're not cycling to Birmingham," I said, "we're going to Market Norton, to get a train."

Her eyes went big. "On a Sunday?"

"Yes!"

"Are you sure?"

"*Yes*." Market Norton was where Darcy used to live. I'd been there on a Sunday. I knew that there were trains. "Look, stop wittering," I said. "You were the one that said to go today. Just get on that bike and let's get started!"

As we rode off, I asked Honey where her mum was. "How did you get out without her seeing you? She *didn't* see you, did she?"

Honey shook her head. "She's asleep. She won't wake up" – Honey and her bike went wobbling slowly towards the hedge at the side of the road – "for ages. Hours, probably. Not till this evening."

I knew what that meant: Mrs de Vito had been at the bottle. That was why Honey had suddenly been so desperate to get out. I'd been there when her mum had come round from one of her binges. Those were the times she was at her meanest, like she was almost blaming Honey for all that had gone wrong, like her husband leaving her for another woman. The awful thing was, Honey was also starting to blame herself. It was right that I'd got her out.

I grabbed hold of her handlebars and yanked her back on to the road.

"Watch it!" I tried not to sound too impatient, cos I knew she couldn't help it. Her sense of balance just wasn't very good. At school she'd been excused from doing gym because of all the times she'd gone and cut her head open or sprained her ankle or even, once, broken her wrist. There's a word for people that aren't well coordinated, only I can't remember what it is.

Yes, I can! It's *dyspraxic*. I once told Darcy this was what Honey suffered from, dyspraxia, and she said, "She's just an idiot." It's true that Darcy was never a very sympathetic kind of person, but we did have fun together.

"Just keep your eyes on the road," I said Honey. "I don't want you falling off. We can't run away if you've got a broken leg!"

She immediately sat bolt upright, pedalling with grim determination, her eyes fixed straight ahead.

"Have you got any money?" I said. I hoped she had! My pathetic little amount wouldn't take us very far. "Have you brought any?"

"Yes." She nodded, vigorously. The bike went veering off again.

"How much?"

"Fifty pounds."

"*What?*"

"Fifty pounds," said Honey.

I stared at her, unbelieving. "Where'd you get fifty pounds from?"

"Took it out my mum's purse."

I was, like, gobsmacked. Honey just didn't do that sort of thing! She was far too timid. She'd even been scared when I'd tried giving her some of the stuff I'd nicked from Woolie's, during my bad-girl period with Darcy. She'd been convinced the police were going to come and arrest her. Now here she was, calmly helping herself to the contents of her mum's purse!

"It's all right." Honey wobbled again; in my direction, this time. "It's not stealing!"

How did she work that out???

"It's only what Mum would have had to spend on me anyway. Like if I was still at home," said Honey. "She'd have to get food for me, and clothes and stuff. So I've just saved her the trouble."

I was quite struck by this argument. It had never occurred to me to see it that way! Honey looked pleased.

"I'd have taken more," she said, "but it was all she had."

I said that it was probably just as well. "Anything over fifty and it starts getting a bit heavy."

She insisted again that it wasn't stealing.

"I wouldn't *steal*. Not from my own mum. I wouldn't steal from anybody! I just took whatever it would have cost if I'd still been there. That's not the same as *stealing*."

I said, "Of course it's not," and "Of course you wouldn't," and "That's absolutely right," but it didn't stop her keeping on about it. She was still going on when we reached Market Norton.

Honey could be maddening like that. She could be maddening in lots of ways, actually. Every now and again it used to get on my nerves and I'd snarl at her – and then immediately wish that I hadn't. Everybody has their faults – I'm sure I have simply loads – but Honey was so sweet, and so good-natured, and so eager to please. I don't remember her ever once being nasty about anyone. She never made unkind remarks, like the rest of us did. I wish I'd been nicer to her! There were lots of times when I was mean. Like for instance when I said that we should dump our bikes in the hedge and walk up the hill to the station, and she gave me this reproachful look and said, "We can't just dump them!"

I said, "Why can't we?"

"Cos that really *would* be stealing," said Honey.

That's when I got mean. I said, "Look, just stop with all this stealing thing, you're driving me nuts! This is my bike, and I can do what I like with it. And that's Kirsty's, and she doesn't even use it any more. In any case, look at the state of it!"

Even then, she had to go and argue with me, saying why couldn't we leave them at the station so they could be found and given back? I snapped, "Cos we don't want them to be found! We're supposed to be *running away*. Right? We don't want them coming after us before we've even got anywhere! For goodness' sake!"

Honey shut up then. We dumped the bikes where I said, and walked on up the hill. Because it was Sunday,

there were hardly any people about. There was no one at all at the station, just me and Honey. According to the indicator board there was a train due in five minutes, and I have to say that that was a great relief. I'd been a bit worried about the trains, to tell the truth, cos they don't have that many on a Sunday. If we'd have missed the 15:18, we'd have had to wait over four hours for the next one. I don't what we'd have done. Gone into hiding, or something. I said to Honey that I thought luck was on our side.

"Incidentally," I said, "did you bring your phone with you?"

She nodded, eagerly.

"Well, just make sure you don't use it," I said. "In fact, give it me! I'll take care of it for you." I had this feeling they could trace people through their mobiles; I was sure I'd seen it on the telly. "It might even be best if we just junked them," I said.

Honey's lip quivered. "Junk our phones?"

"Yes! But wait till we're on the train, we can chuck them out the window. They're no *use* to us," I said. "Not unless you want to get caught and dragged back home again?"

"No!"

"OK, so gimme your phone."

Obediently, she handed it over. I could tell she wasn't happy about it, cos Honey's phone was her pride and joy, but we simply couldn't afford to take any chances.

"Don't worry, we can always get new ones later on," I said.

Honey opened her mouth to say "How?" I knew she was going to say how; all she ever did was ask questions that I couldn't answer. *Extremely* annoying. I told her again not to worry.

"It'll all work out. Look, here's the train!"

The ticket office was closed, which meant we had to buy our tickets on board. I should have told Honey that I would get them for both of us; I just didn't think. It was nearly a disaster! When the ticket man came round and asked us where we were going, Honey went and jumped in before I even had a chance to open my mouth. Very loudly and firmly she said, "I want a ticket to Glasgow!" And then she promptly clapped a hand to her mouth and squawked, "I mean, L—"

"*New Street.*" I got it in just in time. Another second and she'd have blurted it out. "Two singles to New Street."

"Not London?" She whispered it at me, but by then there was no one to hear. The ticket man had gone, and the rest of the train was deserted. "I thought we were going to London!"

I said, "We are, but we don't want him to know."

"Oh." Honey thought about it a while. "In case he tells someone?"

"Yes, cos he's bound to remember us. As soon as he sees our pictures—"

"What pictures?" Honey sounded alarmed.

"The ones they'll put on telly, asking if anyone's seen us. But it's all right! He'll think we're going to Glasgow. *I want a ticket to Glasgow* – oh!" I clapped a hand to my mouth and gazed at her in anguish over the top of it. Honey grinned. "Great bread crumb!" I said.

four

When we got to New Street, I said to Honey that we had to split up. She stared at me, wildly. I could tell she was about to go into panic mode.

"Honey, we have to!" I said. "People will remember if there are two of us." I told her to go off and buy a ticket. "You know what to ask for… a single to London. Yes?"

She nodded, uncertainly.

"Say it!"

"A single to London."

"London Euston."

"London Euston. Then what do I do?"

"Then you follow me down to the platform and we wait for the train. But we have to sit in different compartments. We don't know each other! We're nothing to do with each other. So don't come and talk to me, or anything."

She munched on her lip. "What about when we get there?"

"We get off separately and go through the barrier. You'll know when to get off cos it's the end of the line. The train doesn't go any further."

Still she dithered.

"Look, just do it!" I said. I gave her a little push. The longer we stood around, the more chance there was of someone noticing us. "London Euston!"

Reluctantly, she moved off. I could hear her muttering it to herself: London Euston, London Euston. I waited till a couple more people had joined the queue then slipped in behind, where I could keep an eye on her. I was a bit tensed up, as you never quite knew with Honey. She was just as likely to turn round at the last minute and give a joyous shout of "**LONDON EUSTON**". Fortunately she didn't, but she did flash me this triumphant beam as she walked off with her ticket. I pretended not to know her. I even looked around, making like I was trying to see who she was beaming at.

When my turn came the ticket man eyed me most  suspiciously, like "Why is someone your age buying a ticket to London?" I stared at him, haughtily. What was it to him, how old I was? I had the money. He was just there to sell tickets! In any case, he ought to be glad that I was using the train. We could have thumbed lifts and saved on fares, but I knew not to do that. Getting lifts from strangers was dangerous and irresponsible. I had Honey to think of! He had absolutely *no right* to look at me like I was some kind of delinquent.

I clawed up my ticket and stalked off to look at the departure boards. I'd only been down to London once, with Mum and Dad last year, but it wasn't the first time I'd been to New Street. I knew my way around! I could hear the slop, slap of Honey's sandals close behind me. Too close; she was practically treading on my heels. As

I turned away from the departure boards I almost bumped into her. I hissed, "Keep away! Hang back!"

There was a train at 15:45. Quarter to four in normal speak. We might just catch it if we hurried. I didn't dare to run, or Honey would go and trip over, for sure, but I walked as fast as I could. I heard the slop, slap coming after me and knew she was managing to keep up. I didn't expect her to go and jump on the train *on top of me*, but at least she was on. I pulled an agonised face and mouthed, "Move further down!"

When I wandered along the train a bit later, in search of the loo, I saw Honey sitting scrunched up in a corner seat, clutching her rucksack very tightly with both hands, like she expected someone to snatch it off her at any moment. I wished I could tell her to stop looking so scared. It was a dead give-away! Exactly the sort of thing that would jog people's memories. *A young girl on the train, looking frightened…*

On the way back from the

loo I tried my best not to notice her, but I could feel her eyes kind of boring into me. I shifted my gaze very slightly and gave her this big grin. It was meant to reassure, but as I turned at the end of the compartment, to look back, I saw this pale face, all anguished, and these beseeching eyes fixed on me. I thought, Honey, for goodness' sake!

It wasn't her fault. She had never in her life been to London; I don't think she'd ever even been on a train journey, other than just locally. I knew how timid she was, and how easily things scared her. Just for a minute I was tempted to go and sit with her and tell her that everything was going to be all right. I resisted, however. It wasn't like she was in any danger – unless she did something totally daft, such as getting off the train before we arrived in London. Which surely she wouldn't? Or would she? That was the problem with Honey: you could never be quite certain. I decided that if we stopped anywhere, I would just have to keep a watch out.

I was beginning to realise that having Honey with me was more of a burden than I'd imagined. Not that I resented it; I hardly could. She may have been the one who'd said "Let's go!" but I was the one who'd put the idea in her head. I knew I had to take responsibility.

When the ticket inspector came round I asked him what time we got to Euston and he said five minutes past six. Still almost two hours away! Two hours is a long time to just sit and do nothing. I wished I'd bought some magazines to read, but we'd been in too much of a rush to catch the train. I'm not good at doing nothing; I guess I'm quite an impatient sort of person. Maybe I'd go along to the restaurant car and buy a Coke and a KitKat and check on Honey.

Oh, God! She was talking to someone. A woman, thank heavens; not a man. But bad enough she was talking at all. Goodness only knew what she would be telling them! I turned and she looked up. I gave an angry jerk of the head and set off towards the restaurant car. I heard Honey following me.

"What are you doing?" I hissed. "What are you talking to that woman about?"

Honey said, "Nothing! Her daughter's just had a baby."

"Well, stop it! You're not supposed to be talking to anyone. She'll *remember* you."

Honey's face fell. I immediately felt guilty. No one, but no one, could look as pathetic and crestfallen as Honey.

I said, "Go and sit in another part of the train! And don't talk to *anybody*. Just stay put until we get there."

Honey scuttled away, frightened. I knew I'd been mean, but it had to be done. There was no point laying trails all the way to Glasgow then dropping huge great crumbs that led to London.

I went back to my seat and carefully broke my KitKat into eight pieces. I thought that I would eat one piece every quarter of an hour, until we got there.

It was what I used to do at school when we had a particularly tedious and boring lesson to get through. Maths, for instance. Geography. I'd count out ten Smarties and pop one into my mouth every five minutes, or I'd screw ten scraps of paper into tiny little balls and move them one by one from the right-hand side of my desk to the left, or even just mark off the minutes in my rough book. Pathetic, really, but you have to do something to pass the time.

As I savoured my first bite of KitKat, I wondered if I'd been stupid, asking the ticket inspector what time we arrived. The more I thought about it, the more I thought it had been a really dumb thing to do. I wanted to kick myself! There I was, telling Honey off for drawing attention to us, and I'd gone and done exactly the same thing. After all my planning! I made up my mind that from that moment on I would be doubly cautious and check every single action before I made it. I'd seen enough cop shows to know how the police operated. Once they'd got started on an investigation, they left no stone unturned.

I knew in the end they'd discover we'd gone to London. They'd show our pictures on television, and someone would be bound to recognise us. *Oh, that's the girl that was on the train! That's the girl that bought the ticket.* If I'd really planned it properly, we'd have worn wigs and dark glasses. We'd have had bags full of disguises!

I got quite carried away, thinking up all the different disguises we could have used. All the different wigs and glasses. Dark glasses, ordinary glasses. Funny glasses like you get in joke shops, the sort that make your eyes look as if they're in a goldfish bowl. Funny teeth. Sticky-out ones and pointy ones and great doorstep ones. We could even have stuffed cotton wool in our cheeks, and padded our bras with rolled-up socks.

I fantasised for a bit, seeing myself with a huge inflated bosom and a long blonde wig. I have always fancied having a big bosom. I don't know why; it is just something that appeals. I suppose there is still time, though as Mum has bosoms the size of grapenuts I don't really hold out very much hope.

I looked at my watch, thinking that by now I must

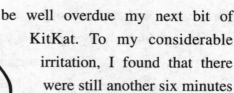

be well overdue my next bit of KitKat. To my considerable irritation, I found that there were still another six minutes to go. How slowly time passed! I couldn't even study other people, which is what I sometimes like to do. I imagine how they might look, for instance, without any clothes on. Not in any rude sort of way. Just, like, whether they would have chest hair or a saggy belly or something. Other times I mentally dress them up in different clothes. I enjoy doing that! I have quite a good dress sense, I think. But today I didn't dare look at anybody for fear of drawing attention. I just stared glumly out of the window and watched the boring countryside flash by.

I ate a second bit of KitKat and tried to get back into my fantasy. Me in a blond wig, with big bosoms! It didn't work. All I could see was me as I am, which is dark-haired and and somewhat on the skinny side. I wondered which photograph they would use when they put us on television. "The two missing teenagers." We'd probably be in the papers, as well. I hoped Mum wouldn't give them my last school photograph. It was me in the netball team, when I'd gone and blinked at just the wrong moment. I'd also, for some weird reason, been waving my lips about, like a horse when it yawns. God, I hoped she didn't give them that one! I wouldn't want that splashed all over the place for everyone to see.

Maybe she'd give them the nice one that Auntie Claire had taken at Christmas. My hair had just been washed, so it was all shiny and bouncy, and I was smiling straight into the camera and looking – though I say it myself – rather like Jennifer Lopez. Actually, I wasn't the one that said it, Auntie Claire was.

"Well, will you look at that! J-Lo's double!"

Dad, of course, hadn't a clue who Jennifer Lopez was, and had to have it explained to him. He was distinctly not impressed; he doesn't rate movie stars. He almost certainly wouldn't let Mum give them my J-Lo photo. He'd make her give them the hideous netball one. A truly depressing thought.

I wondered what Honey was doing. Please God don't let her be talking to anyone! I felt that really I ought to go and check on her again, but I'd already been up and down the train twice, once to the loo and once to the restaurant car. People would start to notice if I wasn't careful.

I gobbled down my next bit of KitKat two minutes early and forced myself to stay in my seat. I tried to picture the scene where Mum and Dad came on television to weep and say how much they loved me and wanted me back. *Please, Jade! Wherever you are… just come back to us!*

Dad would have to say it, too; not just Mum. He would have to say, "All is forgiven." And maybe say he was sorry for the way he'd treated me.

No! Dad would never do that. He wasn't the sort of person to apologise. Even fantasies have to have some sort of basis in reality. Well, mine do. I'd be prepared to settle for him saying that all was forgiven and he wanted me back. If he said that, then maybe I'd go. *Maybe.* Possibly. I'd have to see how things worked out.

After all, we hadn't even got to London yet! Still another forty-two minutes to go...

We got there. At last! As I stood waiting for the doors to open, I saw Honey anxiously lumbering up. *Now* what was she doing? She was supposed to keep her distance! At least I knew she was still on the train; that was some comfort.

I set off up the platform, determinedly not looking back. After a few seconds I heard the familiar slap, slop of her sandals and she appeared, a bit breathless, at my side.

"Is it all right to be together now?"

I said, "Yes, OK." There were loads of people around, even though it was a Sunday. I didn't think anyone was very likely to notice us.

"So what do we do now?"

"We have to find the Underground and get on a tube."

I knew the Underground was somewhere about, cos I could remember using it when I came with Mum and Dad. I'd just forgotten the station was so big. Well, I don't expect it's any bigger than New Street, which is pretty vast, but I know New Street. I didn't know Euston. It was all a bit confusing.

"There's got to be a sign," I said. "Just keep walking!" People would notice if we hung about. We had to look like we knew where we were going.

"Do we *have* to get on a tube?" said Honey.

I said, "Yes! Why?"

"Nothing. I just wondered."

"We've been through all this," I said. "It's what we planned… we'd get the tube. What's the problem?"

Honey hung her head. "There might be bombs."

"Bombs could be anywhere," I said. "This is London! It's where it's all at."

"We should have gone to Glasgow."

"We couldn't go to Glasgow! I already told you. Just shut up! Look, Underground." I pointed. "Over there!"

Honey trailed dismally after me. I said, "I could do with a bit more support here. We are supposed to be in this *together*."

"Sorry." She flailed wildly with her rucksack and almost sent a nearby couple flying. I said, "*Honey!*" You couldn't afford to go round biffing people with rucksacks. Not in London. I'd read about it! You could be knifed or even worse, just for looking at someone. "Just watch it," I said.

"Sorry!" She scuttled after me, down the steps. "I don't think I like it here!"

"Why not? It's exciting," I said. "Things happen! You just have to get used to it. Let's go and find a map."

Even when we'd found the map it took me ages to find Stonebridge Park. Even when I'd found Stonebridge Park I couldn't figure out how to get there. Stonebridge Park was on the brown line while Euston was on the black one and the pale blue one. How did we get on to the brown one??? All the time I'm trying to work it out, Honey's jittering at my elbow and saying that she doesn't think this is such a good idea, and why couldn't we get a bus?

"I like buses! I don't like being underground. I don't

feel safe! I want to get a bus!"

That was when I lost my temper; just slightly. I knew I shouldn't, but I was under a lot of stress and Honey really was not being helpful. I snapped that we couldn't get a bus cos I didn't know where they went from.

"Darcy never said anything about buses! She said to use the tube. If there'd been a bus, she'd have said. Obviously there isn't one."

"There could be," said Honey. "Why don't we ask?" She tugged at my sleeve. "Jade... let's ask!"

"*No.*" How many times did I have to tell her? We couldn't afford to draw attention to ourselves.

While Honey's jittering and I'm trying to trace different coloured lines on the map, a man comes up to us and says, "You look as if you're in trouble. Need any help?" Before I can stop her, Honey's like, "Oh, thank you! Yes! *Please!* We want to find out about buses."

The man laughs at that. I think he looks shifty, though maybe that's just me being suspicious. He tells Honey that she won't find any buses down here. "You'll have to go out to the Euston Road. That's where the buses are. Come on, I'll show you!"

He turns and Honey turns with him. She's actually going to go off with him! A man. A total *stranger*. I grab at her and yank her back.

"It's OK," I say. "We can manage, we're getting the tube."

I turn back to the map and begin tracing lines with my finger. What we need to do is get on the *pale blue* line, which is the Victoria line, as far as Oxford Circus, and then change on to the *brown* line, which is the Bakerloo line, to Stonebridge Park. I feel quite proud of myself! Tube maps are pretty simple, once you get the hang of them. But I've always been good at map reading. It's a sort of gift I have.

"OK!" I swing round to tell Honey. "While you've been wittering on about—"

Honey's not there. She's not there!

"*Honey?*" I shriek, at the top of my voice.

Where has she gone? I can't see her! This is like a nightmare! She's totally disappeared.

And then I catch a glimpse of something blue... Honey's T-shirt. She's going back up the steps with the shifty man. I yell, "*Hunneee!*" and go charging after her, banging and barging and crashing into people.

"*HunnEEEEE!*"

I finally manage to attract her attention. She's already on her way out of the station. The man is pressed right up next to her.

"Honey, stop!" I shout.

Honey looks at me, surprised.

"What's the matter? I'm just finding out about buses."

"We're not getting buses!" I seize her by the arm and haul her back with me, down the steps. Away from the man. She protests, loudly.

"What are you doing? I wasn't going anywhere. I was going to come back!"

I say, "That's what you think," and scuttle off as fast as may be towards the ticket machines, towing Honey with me.

"That was so rude," she says. "He was only trying to help! If you'd just let me find out, we could easily have got a bus. There's loads of them!"

Very slowly, I spell it out for her. "We are *not – getting – a bus*. Read my lips: *no bus*. We are getting the *tube*."

Honey mutters that she doesn't want to get a tube. I say well, too bad, cos we're getting one.

"And don't ever do that to me again!"

"Do what?" says Honey.

"Go off with some stranger!"

"He was only going to show me where the buses were."

"How do you know? This is *London,* he could have abducted you. You could have ended up in a dark alley with your throat cut. Then how d'you think I'd feel?"

This frightens her, so that for a few seconds she is humble and silent, but perks up again as we buy our tickets.

"Shall I get a child's one?" She giggles. "I could be under sixteen!"

I nearly say yes, cos I can't see anyone's likely to challenge her. She really does act young for her age, specially when she's not sure of herself. I, on the other hand, have always acted far older than I am. It's one of the things that Dad and I have had some of our most bitter rows about.

"*Shall* I?" says Honey. "It'd save us money!"

I'm tempted, but in the end I tell her no, it's not worth it. I remind her that we can't afford to take any unnecessary risks.

"Oh, well, OK," she says, and giggles again. "I'll be sixteen!"

She gets another dose of the wobbles when we discover that there's a Victoria line southbound and a Victoria line northbound and we can't immediately decide which one to go for, but then I read the list of stations and find Oxford Circus on the southbound bit, so that's all right. I do believe that I am quite a practical sort of person. I enjoy finding my way round strange places, I look upon it as a challenge.

I slip my arm through Honey's. I suddenly feel incredibly fond of her, and protective.

"See?" I give her a squeeze. "Everything's working out really well!"

five

It was seven o'clock when we got on the brown line at Oxford Circus. We had been gone for almost five hours, though it actually felt a lot longer. Mum, and Dad, and home, seemed like really far away. I could have found it a bit scary, if I'd let myself. I knew that I had to keep focused. So long as I concentrated on getting us to Darcy's, I was OK; I had something to aim for. It was when I stopped to look back that little shivers of doubt came creeping in. I couldn't afford to have doubts! I had Honey to take care of.

She was sitting next to me, clutching her rucksack tightly with both hands.

"It's going to be OK," I said. "There's nothing to worry about."

"I'm not worried," said Honey. "So long as we're together."

No one was going to separate us, that was for sure.

I knew, when we got to Stonebridge Park, that I would have to break the rules and ask someone for directions. I really didn't want to, cos it was almost Rule no.1, *Don't talk to anybody*, but I hadn't the faintest idea how to get from the station to Darcy's place.

"You didn't ask her?" said Honey.

I said, "No, how could I? I haven't spoken to her!"

Honey turned slowly to look at me. "You haven't even told her we're coming?"

"I didn't have a chance! It was all such a rush. Anyway, I don't know her telephone number." Her mobile had stopped working ages ago, and if she had an email address she'd never given it to me. She'd texted me a couple of times, when she'd first gone down to London, but after that it had just been postcards. Well, just one postcard, actually, saying how cool it was, being only thirty minutes from the West End.

"It's all right," I said, "there's no problem. She told me, if ever I wanted a place to crash – like if ever it got too heavy at home and I had to get out – she told me, I could always just turn up."

"That's you," said Honey. "What about me?"

"Both of us! It's OK, she won't mind."

"If she's still there," muttered Honey.

"Look, will you *please* just stop being so negative all the time!" I stamped my foot, in a way I now see was rather childish. I mean, Honey did have a point. For all I knew, Darcy's sister could have moved to the other side of London, taking Darcy with her. They might not even be in London; they could be anywhere in the country. I'd been purposely not thinking about it. There is absolutely nothing to be gained from worrying yourself to a frazzle about things which might never happen. Cross your bridges when you come to them, is my motto.

It was distinctly annoying that Honey, of all people, should start carping and criticising. She couldn't plan her way out of a paper bag.

Urgently, she said, "I don't want to go home again!"

"We're not going home again." Not yet, anyway.

"If I went home, I could be done for stealing!"

I reminded her what she had said. "You told me it wasn't stealing."

Honey munched on her lip. "They'd say it was."

"Then we'd tell them it wasn't. Come on, this is our stop!" I jumped up. "Another ten minutes and we'll be at Darcy's."

There weren't very many people about, not like at Euston, but I saw an old lady coming towards us and I thought that she would be a good person to ask. Old people don't always see too well, and they don't always remember things, either. Like one of my granddads, who can't remember names. He says things like, "You know wotsisname? That chap who's on that programme on the telly. The one about wotsit. Thingummy and wotsit." Sometimes it's quite funny; even Granddad has a laugh. But just to be on the safe side, cos some old people can be quite sharp, I told Honey to go back into the station and wait.

"I'll just find out where to go. Don't move!"

"I'm not going anywhere," said Honey. She said it with this air of injured dignity, like I'd insulted her. But sometimes you had to treat her like a child; she'd be just as likely to go wandering off and get herself lost.

The old lady wasn't as old as I'd first thought, so it was just as well I'd told Honey to wait. I asked, in this really posh voice, if she could tell me where Durden Way was. I can do a posh voice, no problem; I can talk like the Queen, if I want. If anybody asked her, the old lady would probably reckon I was one of those sophisticated London types. She wouldn't ever connect me with a fourteen-year-old girl gone missing from Birmingham! She told me how to get to Durden Way, and I thanked her and went whizzing back to collect Honey, who was waiting obediently inside the station.

"Come on!" I said. "It's not far."

We set off, up the road.

"This isn't a very nice place, is it?" said Honey.

I said that it was all right. I said, "Anything's better, I should have thought, than being back home with your mum."

"Or with your dad," said Honey.

"Yeah, or with my dad. Quick, before the lights change!"

I snatched at her arm and dragged her with me across the road. It was a wide road, with traffic thundering in both directions. I know it sounds pathetic, but I wasn't used to busy roads. Only when I went in to Birmingham, which didn't happen very often. I guess I misjudged it. I shouldn't have hustled her, I knew what Honey was like. As we reached the kerb on the far side she tripped, and went sprawling. I thought, "Oh, God, why does she have to be so *clumsy* all the time?" But it wasn't her fault. It was mine, if anyone's.

"Honey?" I took her hand, to pull her up. "Are you OK?"

"No." Her eyes filled with tears. She was always someone who cried easily, but it did seem like she was in real pain.

"What is it?" I said. "What have you done?"

"I've hurt my ankle!"

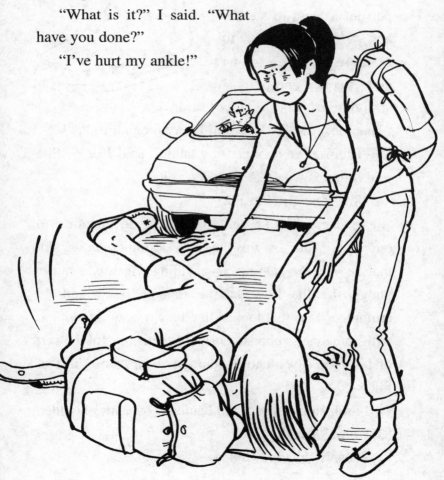

"How bad? Can you walk?"

She shook her head.

"Try!" I said.

"I can't, it hurts!"

She wobbled, and I put out a hand to steady her. I bent down, to examine her ankle. It was quite swollen and puffy. As I straightened up, a voice said, 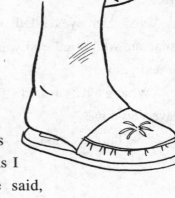 "That looked nasty, that did! Everything all right?"

"I think I've sprained my ankle," said Honey. She said it in this woeful, tear-laden voice.

"She'll be OK," I said.

We weren't supposed to be drawing attention to ourselves! And now this boy was looming over us. Not that he was threatening, or anything. He was a rather pudgy, slob-like boy, wearing a baggy T-shirt and old crumpled jeans that looked like they'd been thrown out with someone's rubbish. Distinctly uncool. Not the sort of boy you'd want to encourage, even at the best of times.

I took Honey's arm and hauled it over my shoulder. "Try now," I said.

"I can't!" wailed Honey.

"She can't," said the boy. "Let me!" He put his arm round Honey's waist and half carried her across the pavement. "You'd best come in and sit down," he said. "Have a cuppa tea, make you feel better."

"Oh, yes, please! I'd like that," said Honey.

Talk about playing up! She doesn't even drink tea. I followed, fretfully, as the boy helped her through the door of this greasy spoon type café that he'd obviously come out of.

"You sit yourself down," he said, "I'll get you a cuppa. Hot and sweet! Do you good."

Honey gave this tremulous smile. I could see the pudgy boy practically going to jelly. Honey had this effect on boys. *Some* boys; not all of them. Soper, for instance. Soper liked girls that were sparky and fought back. But soft boys, like old Slobbo in his crumpled jeans, they just melted. I don't think Honey was even aware of it. She was a true innocent.

I parked myself impatiently on the edge of a plastic chair. Old pudgy Slobbo asked me if I would like something to drink, and I told him – not quite as graciously as I might have done – that I didn't want anything, thank you. We were in a hurry!

"I'll try walking again in a minute," said Honey.

Slobbo had come back with her cup of tea. The colour of engine oil. Yuck! I don't know how people drink the stuff. He told Honey to "Get that down you.

Stop you going into shock."

Oh, please! All she'd done was just trip over her own feet.

"I'm Joe." He beamed at her; a big sloppy beam. Honey twinkled back at him. "I'm H—"

Just in time, I banged my rucksack on to the table. "She's Harriet," I said loudly. "I'm Lucy."

I don't know why I chose those particular names; they were just the first that came to mind. Honey's mouth fell open, and she turned slowly scarlet. Then, in a rush, she said, "Yes! I'm Harriet and she's Lucy."

"Do you think, when you've drunk that tea, we'll be able to get on?" I said.

Honey munched on her lip. "I don't know!"

"Depends how far you're going," said Joe.

Honey turned to look at me. "Not far," I said. And then, reluctantly, since there didn't seem to be any alternative, I added, "Durden Way."

"Doubt she'll get that far," said Joe. "Not without a bit of help."

Desperation made me bold. "Maybe you could help her?" I said.

"Have to give me half an hour," said Joe. "Can't leave the caff. Got to wait till my nan comes back."

I sat there, fuming. Like I said, I am rather an impatient kind of person. I waited till Joe had gone off to serve someone, then whispered urgently to Honey, "I need to go and check that Darcy's there! Will you be OK if I leave you and come back?"

"Yes!" Honey smiled, bravely, at me.

"You sure you don't mind?"

"No, I'll just sit here and drink my tea."

"OK, well – *don't tell him anything.* I'll be back as soon as I can."

I didn't see how even Honey could get into trouble sitting at a table in a café, in full view of anyone who happened to pass by. Plus there were other people in there. Plus I'd only be gone about half an hour.

I shot off up the road. I was suddenly terrified in case Darcy wasn't there. Why hadn't I written to her, to find out? I'd told Honey it was because everything had happened in such a mad rush, but that wasn't strictly true. It might have been a bit of a rush, just at the end, when Dad had been so cold and hateful, but the idea had been buzzing about my brain for ages. If Dad didn't stop picking on me, I was getting out! I was leaving home! But right up until the actual moment when I wheeled the bikes out of the garage, it had been more of a game than anything else. A way of getting back at Dad; of plotting my revenge. Now, pounding up an alien street all by myself, it had become reality, and I wasn't quite sure that I liked it.

I was even less sure when I finally turned into Durden Way and discovered that where Darcy lived was a big block of flats. Tall, and grey, and forbidding. I reminded myself that this was London: this was how people lived, in London. London was where it was all at, and it was exciting!

It was also a bit scary. Fortunately, being summer, it was still light, but I did wish Honey were with me.

The address I had for Darcy was 3.11, Gladstone House. I'd never really stopped to think what 3.11 actually meant, but I managed to work out that 3 must be the number of the floor and 11 was the number of the flat. I felt quite pleased with myself. I hadn't had to ask! Not that there was anyone around that I could have asked, but what I'm saying is, I'd kept my head. I didn't panic!

I got into the lift and pressed the button and got out at the third floor. I still hadn't met a single, solitary person. I might as well admit it, my heart was banging like mad. I hadn't ever been in a big block of flats before; it was a bit like a prison. How I imagine a prison. This long, dark passageway, without any windows; just endless rows of doors, and graffiti scribbled on the walls. I found number 11 and pressed the bell. What were we going to do if Darcy wasn't there???

But she was! I have never been so relieved in all my life as when the door opened and I saw her standing there.

"*Jade*! Hey, wow, I can't believe it!"

I said, "Darce? Is it OK?"

"Sure, sure! Come in."

I followed her inside. "I know I should have asked first, but—"

"No prob!"

"You did say, if ever—"

"No problem!"

Darcy was one of those people, she just took everything in her stride. Like I could have turned up in the middle of the night and she'd still have said "Come in." Nothing ever fazed Darcy.

"So what's happened? You haven't—" She stopped, and peered at me. "My God, you have!"

"I have," I said. "I've finally done it… I've left!"

"Cool," said Darcy. "That's cool. About time, too! I don't know how you stood it so long!"

I said, "Neither do I. He just made my life impossible."

"I'd have done it yonks ago," said Darcy.

"I kept thinking about it. But then he was just so – so *squalid*. Like Mum wanted me to go and apologise to him, even though I hadn't actually done anything to apologise for, but I did it anyway, I told him I was sorry—"

"That was your first mistake," said Darcy.

"I wanted to keep Mum happy, but he was so horrible I couldn't take it any more. I just grabbed my stuff and ran."

"Best way."

"But it's all right, I've covered our tracks! I made it look like we've gone to Glasgow." I giggled. "I've laid clues on the computer! I—"

"Hang about, hang about!" said Darcy. "Who's *we*?"

"Me and Honey."

"*Honey*? Honey de Vito? Are you out of your mind? What d'you wanna go and bring her for?"

"I had to! I couldn't come without her. Her mum is just so mean, you have no idea! She needed to get away even more than I did."

"So where is she?"

"She's gone and done her ankle in. I've left her in that café place down on the main road."

"Soup 'n Sarnies? You've left her with Fat Joe?"

"Yes. Why? He's all right," I said, "isn't he?"

"Yeah, he's just an idiot. But so's she, so that makes two of 'em!"

Earnestly I said, "Honey's not an idiot, it's just that she gets nervous and then she loses it."

"Yeah, yeah! Whatever." Darcy waved a hand. "So what's gonna happen to her? She staying with Fatso?"

"No, I said I'd go back and get her. You don't mind, do you?"

"I don't give a rat's bum," said Darcy. "You're the one that's saddled with her."

"What about your sister?"

"She's not here, she's gone off for a few days with her bloke."

"She's left you on your own?"

"Yeah, with the baby."

"*Baby?*"

I squawked it at her. Darcy gave this loud guffaw. "You should see your face!" She let her mouth hang open and her eyes go like dinner plates. "*Baby?* Not mine, you dumbo! Hers. Catch me having a baby. No thank you!"

"So she's left you to look after it?"

"Yeah, worse luck. She said it's the price I have to pay for being allowed to move in with her. It's still a darn sight better than living with my mum. You ever see my mum these days?"

"No." I shook my head.

"Got herself a new man, last I heard."

I couldn't help feeling that it would be nice for Darcy's mum, to have a man. A *new* man. The last one she'd had had knocked her about, and she didn't deserve that. She was ever so little and thin and timid. To be honest, I never thought Darcy was that kind to her, but I didn't ever say so. It didn't seem my place.

"Well—" I hesitated. "Maybe I'd better go and check on Honey, see if she's OK. I'll bring her back with me, yeah?"

"Yeah, can't wait," said Darcy.

I found Honey where I had left her, sitting at her table near the window, with Joe. They had their heads together and didn't even bother to look up as I appeared. Pointedly I said, "*Harriet*." That made her jump.

"Oh!" she said. "Lucy!" And then she gave Joe this sly little look and giggled.

I said, "Can you walk yet?"

"It's all right." Joe pushed back his hair. "I'll help her. I'll just tell my nan. Nan!" He bellowed through a doorway. "I'm off out for a few minutes."

"She came back," said Honey.

Joe walked with us as far as Gladstone House, with Honey hanging on his arm. I wasn't totally convinced that she needed his support, but she was obviously basking in it. I reckoned by now she'd have gone and blurted out everything, all about Darcy, and how we were at school together, and how we were going to stay in the flat with her. She was such a blabbermouth! At least old fatso didn't come into the building with us. I think he would have done, if I'd let him, but I very firmly said that we could manage OK, now.

"There's a lift."

"Right. Well." He looked at Honey. What I call a soppy sort of look. "You know where I am if you need me."

"Why should we need him?" I said, as I helped Honey across the entrance hall.

"He was just being nice," said Honey.

He probably was, and I was being mean, but I was just so angry that we'd drawn attention to ourselves.

"If he sees us on the telly," I said, "he'll recognise us, for sure!"

Honey looked alarmed. "We're going to be on television?"

"Our pictures will be. And he'll go straight to the police!"

"I could always ask him not to."

"How can you ask him not to? You won't be seeing him again!" I bustled her into the lift. "We're not supposed to be talking to anybody." Honey was so dejected that to cheer her up I told her about Darcy saying it was OK for us to be there.

"She's cool about it. No problem!"

I also told her about Darcy's sister having gone off and left Darcy in charge of the baby. Honey at once wanted to know how old the baby was, and whether it was a girl or a boy, and what it was called. I said I hadn't asked, and she looked at me, unbelieving.

"You didn't *ask*?"

"You can ask her yourself," I said. "I'm not interested in people's babies. She wants to see it," I said, as Darcy let us in.

"The baby? She can have it if she wants!" Darcy gave another of her cackles. "I'll sell it to you... how much you offering?"

"You can't sell *babies*," said Honey.

"Wanna bet? It's in there." She pointed at a door. "For God's sake, don't wake it up! It's been bawling all evening, I've just managed to get it to sleep."

"Poor little thing! Babies don't cry for no reason," said Honey. "What's its name?"

"Flower."

I said, "*Flour?*"

"Yeah, tell me about it." Darcy rolled her eyes.

"It's beautiful," said Honey.

I didn't know whether she meant the name or the baby. It looked like a pretty dead ordinary sort of baby

to me, but then I am not what you would call an expert.

"Now *she's* here," said Darcy, nodding at Honey, "you and me could go out, yeah?"

I said, "Out where?"

"Anywhere! I've got some mates live just ten minutes away. Go and see them, if you like."

"What, and leave Honey?"

"Why not? She didn't seem to mind being left with Fatso."

"I dunno." I looked at Honey, doubtfully. "Would that be OK?"

Honey swallowed. I could tell she wasn't happy.

"Oh, for heaven's sake!" Darcy was an even more impatient kind of person than I was; she had what Mum calls *a short fuse*. I always used to try and keep on the good side of her. "Just forget about it! We'll leave the baby here, and we'll all go."

"Leave the baby?" squeaked Honey.

"Yeah, it's OK, we'll only be out a couple of hours. I left it last night, nothing happened to it."

"You can't leave the baby!"

"I just told you: I *did*. It's not gonna go anywhere!"

Honey munched on her lip.

"Look, it's all right," I said. "Me and Honey'll stay here and babysit, while you go out and see your friends. We're pretty tired anyway, aren't we?"

Honey nodded, eagerly.

"OK." Darcy shrugged. "If that's what you want."

It wasn't, especially; I'd quite like to have gone out and met people. But even I could see that it wasn't right to leave a small baby, and I couldn't leave Honey. Not on our first night.

"I'll shoot, then," said Darcy. "Help yourselves to food and stuff. I'll see you later."

She flapped a hand, and was gone. Me and Honey were on our own...

six

It was kind of a weird evening. We started off by looking in the fridge, but there wasn't anything much there, just a hunk of mouldering cheese and a festering mess of something we couldn't identify in a plastic pot, so we ended up opening a can of ravioli we found in the cupboard, and did some bits of toast. I watched television while I ate, hopping madly through the channels in case there was any news about me and Honey, but there didn't seem to be. I guessed it was still too soon. I once read that you had to be gone forty-eight hours before you were officially classed as missing. I wondered if Dad would even have contacted the police yet or whether he would be fuming at home, waiting to chew me out. Of course, he might still be at Auntie Claire's and not even know that I had gone. Honey's mum would be asleep, and even when she woke she'd just think that Honey was round at my place. I thought that perhaps, after all, Honey had been right and Sunday was a *good* day for leaving home.

Halfway through the evening the baby started up again. Honey cried, "Oh, the poor little thing!" and went rushing off in a frenzy to see to it. I went on channel hopping. Babies weren't my scene, so if Honey wanted to play nursemaid that was fine by me. Just so long as I didn't have to! A few minutes later, she reappeared, bringing the baby with her.

"I changed it," she said.

I said, "What for? A different model?"

"Its *nappy*," said Honey.

She sat down next to me, on the saggy sofa. I zapped to yet another channel.

"Sooner you than me." Secretly, I thought it was quite brave of her. Catch me changing babies' nappies! I guess I would if I had to, but it wouldn't exactly fill me with joy.

"If this was my baby," said Honey, "I wouldn't go

off and leave it."

"People have to be allowed to get away *sometimes*," I said.

"Not just to go off with a bloke."

"Why not? What's wrong with it?"

"Trusting someone like *Darcy*?"

"She seems to have managed OK so far."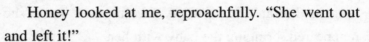

Honey looked at me, reproachfully. "She went out and left it!"

"Only for a couple of hours. If people can go out and leave dogs, I don't see why they can't go out and leave babies."

"Because babies aren't dogs," said Honey.

"Ho! Well. That's a brilliant observation," I said.

I zapped back again, through the channels. Honey retreated, with her bundle, to the far corner of the sofa. I'd obviously upset her.

"You don't have to get all in a huff," I said. I leaned across, trying to think of something nice to say about

the baby. Nothing came to me. "It's not very pretty," I said, "is it?"

"Poor little thing," said Honey.

"It's actually quite ugly."

"That's all the more reason for loving it!" Honey cradled it, protectively.

I shook my head and went back to my channel hopping. Honey had always had a tendency to croon. Mostly over little furry things, such as fieldmice and moles, but sometimes not so furry things, as well. She was the only person I ever knew that rescued slugs. I wished I'd hardened my heart and gone with Darcy.

After a bit the baby started to crumple its hands and cry again.

"God, what's the matter with it?" I said. "It surely can't have done something else?"

"I think it's hungry," said Honey. "Look!" She stuck a finger in its mouth and it immediately started sucking. "It is, it's hungry! Poor little thing. It needs its bottle."

"It can't do," I said. "Darcy would have told us."

Honey said, "*Her?* What would she know?"

"More than we do! She's the one that's looking after it. Where are you going?"

"I'm going to feed it," said Honey.

She headed off towards the kitchen. I sprang up from the sofa and raced after her.

"You can't feed someone else's baby!"

"Yes, I can," said Honey.

"You can't, you don't know what to give it! You might give it the wrong stuff, you might – *what are you doing?*"

"Take her." She thrust the baby at me. "And stop calling her *it*."

"It's what you've been calling her!"

"Only cos you have. But it's not right!"

I watched in growing apprehension as Honey bustled about the kitchen.

"I'm going to go back in the other room," I said.

I took the baby, still crying, and sat stiffly with it in front of the television. I wondered if Honey had gone mad. I wasn't used to her being all bossy and overbearing; she was usually so meek.

When she came back, she was holding a bottle.

"Is that milk?" I said.

"No, it's washing-up liquid. What d'you think?" She took the baby from me and put the bottle to its mouth. Its lips closed over it, greedily. I can't bear this, I thought. This is someone else's baby!

In despairing tones, I said, "I didn't think you could give babies ordinary cows' milk."

Honey stayed silent.

"Not tiny babies," I said.

More silence. Growing desperate I said, "Did you sterilise the bottle? I'm sure you have to sterilise the bottle!"

"I picked it out the rubbish bin," said Honey. "And I told you, it's not milk, it's washing-up liquid."

Oh, God! Now she was being sarcastic.

I said, "All right, you don't have to come off your hinges."

"Well, but honestly! What d'you take me for? An idiot?"

Humbly, I said I hadn't realised she knew so much about babies. I said, "How come? Where'd you learn all this stuff?"

"It's just something you know," said Honey.

It wasn't anything I knew, and I had a sister. Not that I could really remember Kirsty as a baby, but Honey didn't have anyone; she was an only child. I looked at her with new respect. This was a side of her I'd never seen before.

The baby settled once it had had its bottle. Honey took it back to its crib while I went on with my channel hopping. Anxiously, as she came back, Honey said, "Have they shown us yet?"

"No, it's too early. They might not even know we've gone! I can't remember what time Mum and Dad were coming back from my Auntie's, and your mum's probably still in a drunken stupor."

Honey flushed. "She was asleep."

I said, "Yeah, well. Whatever."

Honey would never admit that her mum drank too much; she was incredibly loyal. I'm not sure I would have been, though I suppose you can't really tell until it happens to you. Honey curled up next to me, on the sofa.

"How long do you think we'll have to stay here?"

"Dunno. Until things work out, I guess."

"Work out how?"

How would I know how? "Just… wait and see what happens."

"I thought we had a plan!"

"We had a plan for getting away. After that—"

"What?"

"I don't know. Stop keeping on! I've got us here, haven't I?"

"But what about money?"

"We'll get some!"

Honey opened her mouth to say "How?" I knew she was going to say how. I thought, "I shall scream!"

"We'll get jobs," I said.

"How?" said Honey.

Very slowly, I counted up to ten.

"I could get a job," said Honey. "I don't think you could, at your age."

The cheek of it! I was far more competent than she was.

"I can always pretend to be older," I said. "I could pass for sixteen any day! You're the one that's likely to have difficulties... trying to buy a *children's* ticket!"

The minute I'd said it, I felt mean. After all, she was the one who'd taken care of the baby.

"Look, just don't worry," I said. "I'll ask Darcy. She'll know!"

I couldn't ask Darcy that night because she didn't come in. At eleven o'clock me and Honey got tired and went to bed. We couldn't decide whether to sleep on the sofa or in the single bed in the baby's room. The bed obviously belonged to Darcy's sister, and we were a bit worried in case she might not like two strange girls sleeping in it; but as I said, "She's not here, so she needn't ever know." And as Honey said, "The baby might wake up and need something."

We'd only been asleep about an hour when there was a banging at the front door. I sprang up, in alarm. Honey clutched at me.

"Don't answer it!"

"But s'ppose it's Darcy?" I said. "She might have gone without her key."

I opened the door just the tiniest crack, keeping the chain on. Two hoodies stood there. A big black one and a weedy white one. They wanted to know if Sharleen was in. I couldn't immediately think who Sharleen was, and then I remembered she was Darcy's sister. In quavering tones I said that she was away, and stood, heart pounding, waiting for the door to be battered down. Instead, after mumbling at each other in their hoods, they said OK and went off again. I closed the door, with trembling hands. Honey, who had been anxiously peering over my shoulder, said, "We could have been murdered!"

It was no more than I had been thinking myself, but one of us had to show some backbone. Very firmly, I told her that that was nonsense.

"Just because one of them was black… you're being really prejudiced!"

Honey said it was nothing to do with being prejudiced. "They were wearing *hoods*."

"Yeah," I said, "it's a fashion statement."

"But it's midnight!" wailed Honey. "Who comes knocking on people's doors at midnight?"

I said, "You're not very streetwise, are you? This is London! They do that sort of thing in London. It's the way they live. It's *different* down here."

"But what did they want?"

"I don't know! They probably wanted to go clubbing, or something."

Honey muttered again about it being midnight. "And Sunday!" I thought pityingly that she had no idea. As we clambered back into bed, she said, "Do you think they'll have discovered we're gone yet?"

"Bound to, by now," I said. People in London might still be wandering round at midnight, but not in Steeple Norton. Especially not teenagers. My curfew was ten o'clock, tops, and that was Fridays and Saturdays. Sunday I was meant to be in by nine thirty. We'd had so many rows about it, I'd lost count. But midnight was unheard of, even for me, so I reckoned Mum and Dad would be pretty sure I'd gone. They'd be asking themselves, "Where can she be?" and "Why did she do it?" Mum might even be crying. Dad—

I couldn't picture what Dad would be doing. He certainly wouldn't be crying. Would he even be worried? Or would he just say, "Good riddance!" and lock the door?

He'd have rung Honey's mum, to check whether I was there – or, more likely, Mum would have rung her. They would have woken her from her stupor and she would have reported that Honey, too, was missing. Maybe Dad would have got into the car and driven round a bit, looking for me. Maybe Mum would have found Marnie's number and tried ringing her. I wondered what Marnie would have said. Would she have told Mum about the boys from Glasgow? Would Dad have rung the police? I could just hear him, bawling them out. Yelling at them to "Shift yourselves and do something!" Dad always came on heavy; he didn't seem to realise he put people's backs up. Maybe he just couldn't help himself.

Darcy must have come back some time during the night, cos when we woke up next morning she was there, in her bedroom, asleep. The baby was crying fit to bust, but Darcy didn't stir. Honey, very indignant, said, "Just as *well* we're here. Poor little thing!" I left Honey to look after her and went to wake Darcy. I bounced myself down on to the bed.

"Hey!" I prodded at her. She groaned, and opened an eye.

"Wozzamadder?"

I said, "The baby's crying."

"Oh, God!" She rolled over, on to her back. "Can't you see to it?"

"Honey is, but I just thought you ought to know."

"Why? What do I want to know for?"

I said, "It's your baby!"

"It's not *my* baby."

"Well, your sister's. Two men called last night," I said.

"Yeah?"

"Midnight. I told them she wasn't here."

"Right." Darcy hauled the duvet over herself.

"Neither were you," I said. "What happened?"

"Nothing happened, I just stayed on a bit. It's half term! You don't have to look at me like that, I wouldn't have gone out if you hadn't been here. I told you, I never leave it more than a couple of hours. OK?"

I said, "OK," though I didn't really think it was. I thought that Honey was right, and if I had a baby I wouldn't trust it to someone like Darcy. But I didn't want to get on the wrong side of her.

There wasn't much for breakfast; just a bit of stale cereal and a couple of crusts of toast. Darcy said that was all right, she wasn't hungry.

"I never eat breakfast." She said she'd go down the shops later on and stock up. "You two had better stay here, you don't want people recognising you. Let's see if you're on the telly!"

We still weren't. I didn't know whether I felt more disappointed or relieved, but Darcy said it was good.

"Longer they leave it, the better." She said that when she came back from shopping she would do something to change our appearances. "Do something with your hair... give it a make-over!"

We had some fun, that first morning. Darcy came back from the shops with a load of chocolate-covered doughnuts, which we sat and consumed straight away. Darcy said, "See if the baby wants some," but Honey wouldn't. She said that doughnuts weren't good for babies.

"They rot the teeth."

Darcy said, "What teeth?" and we both cackled.

Honey got quite cross. She told us that we were behaving irresponsibly. She said, "This baby is *helpless*. We're supposed to be taking care of her."

"Oh, just stop being such a bore," said Darcy. "Me and Jade left home to get away from all that!"

It was true that at home I couldn't have gorged on doughnuts, specially not chocolate-covered ones, without Mum nagging at me. I said this to Darcy.

"This is it," said Darcy. "You're *free*!" She pushed the box of doughnuts at me. "Have another!"

I managed four, but after that I came over a bit sick and had to stop. Darcy jeered and called me a wimp. She said, "You ain't got no stamina, girl! You'd better get your act together tonight, I got hotpot."

"She can't eat hotpot," said Honey. "Not if it's got meat in it. She's a vegetarian."

If looks could have killed, then surely Honey would have dropped dead on the spot. What business was it of hers?

"You gotta be joking," said Darcy.

"No, she is," insisted Honey.

Darcy looked at me like I was some kind of bug-eyed alien. "Since when?"

"Since never," I said. "It was just something to annoy Dad. He got on my nerves, you know? Always trying to make me eat stuff I didn't want."

"You told me it was principle," said Honey.

She was really starting to get on my nerves! Ever since she'd taken charge of the baby, she'd become all bumptious and full of herself.

"It was principle," I said. "Principle of being allowed to decide for myself what I wanted to eat."

Honey opened her mouth. She got as far as, "You s—" when Darcy scrunched up the doughnut box and chucked it at her.

"Never mind all that! Let's get on with the make-over. We'll do Jade first, then you."

She made me sit on a chair in the middle of the room while she slowly walked round, studying me from every angle.

"Know what?" she said. "It's all gotta come off... all that hair! I'll go get the clippers."

Honey looked at me, wonderingly. "Are you going to let her?"

"Course she is!" Darcy's voice sang out from the bathroom. "I know about these things."

It was true, Darcy had always been like a sort of icon where anything to do with fashion was concerned. She came waltzing back, with a pair of clippers.

"It's a total mess, anyway," she said, yanking at a strand of my hair. "Dunno when you last had this lot styled."

I didn't like to tell her that Mum had always cut it. I just mumbled that it was "Ages ago."

"Yeah, that figures," said Darcy.

By the time she'd finished, the floor was covered in wads of hair and I was practically bald. Just a lovely sleek fuzz all over. I gazed wonderingly at myself in the mirror. Mum would never have let me shave my head! Dad would go ballistic.

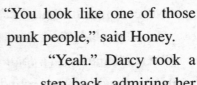

"You look like one of those punk people," said Honey.

"Yeah." Darcy took a step back, admiring her handiwork. "Suits you," she said.

It did, too! I don't mean to brag, but I'd never realised before what a nice shape head I had. Some people, you can't help noticing – like men when they have lost their hair – have heads that are lumpy and bumpy. There are square heads, and pointy heads, and heads like big nobbly potatoes. Mine is quite small, and round, and neat. I am aware that makes me sound like a rather vain sort of person, but it just happens to be true!

"OK," said Darcy. "Now it's her turn."

She moved across to Honey, with the clippers. Honey shrank back, in instant alarm.

"I don't want my hair shaved off!"

"No. Wouldn't suit you," said Darcy. "You've got the wrong sort of face. Too big. What you need…"

"W—what?" said Honey.

"You need a different colour!"

Darcy went rushing off again, down the hall. Honey curled herself up, into a corner of the sofa.

"It's got to be done," I said. "Otherwise we'll never be able to go out."

"Got it!" Darcy burst back into the room, triumphantly clutching a bottle. "Ever wanted to be a brunette?"

"Not really," said Honey.

"Well, you're gonna be! C'mon!"

Between us, we marched Honey into the bathroom and set to. Ten minutes later, her hair was a deep, rich chestnut.

"What d'you reckon?" said Darcy.

"Great," I said. "It matches her eyes."

Honey stared doubtfully at herself in the bathroom mirror. It's funny, cos she looked a whole lot older with her hair dark. Not as striking, but definitely more like sixteen than twelve. I said this to her, thinking she'd be pleased, but she munched on her lip and muttered that, "I don't feel like me."

I said, "That's the whole point! You're not you.

You're a new person. We both are!"

Honey went on munching. Darcy said, "It's no big deal. It only lasts a week or two. If you don't like it, you can always try something else."

"You'll get used to it," I said.

As for me, I preened like mad the rest of the day. Every time I passed a mirror, I had to look in it. I said to Darcy that it had been worth running away, just to get a new hairstyle.

That, of course, is very shallow, and I know that I should be ashamed of ever having such a frivolous thought, especially when Mum was probably sitting at home worried out of her mind, wondering where I was and whether I was all right.

I did feel a bit guilty when I thought of Mum, but only a bit. She had never properly stood up for me. If she had just occasionally been on my side, I could have put up with Dad and his bullying ways. I hadn't *wanted* to run away. Though now that I had, it seemed they didn't really miss me. There still wasn't anything on the

TV news, which surely there ought to have been? It was over twelve hours since we'd left home! Didn't they care? Didn't they want us to be found?

I could see that Honey's mum mightn't be that bothered if she never got Honey back. I could see that my dad, because of his pride and always being convinced he was in the right, might wash his hands of me. I could even see that Kirsty might not be too broken up. But surely Mum still loved me???

Maybe what it was, Mum would have wanted to go to the police and Dad wouldn't let her. Mum would be crying and begging him. "Alec, please! We've got to get her back!" And he'd be, like, "She chose to go, she can stay gone."

I said to Honey, as we lay in bed that night, "I bet that's what it is. I bet Mum's desperate and Dad's bullying her, same as usual."

"What about my mum?" said Honey. "What d'you think she's doing?"

I said, "Drinking, probably." And then, in case that might be hurtful, I added that it wasn't her mum's fault. "People can't help being alcoholics. It's something in their blood."

"She's not an alcoholic!" said Honey. "It's for her nerves."

It would have seemed unkind to argue with her. "Either way," I said, "she can't help it. Let's go to sleep!"

Maybe tomorrow there would be something on the news.

seven

There wasn't anything! Not even so much as a mention. It was like me and Honey simply didn't exist any more. They were just getting on with their lives without us.

"They don't always put things on the telly," said Darcy. "They never did with me."

"You didn't run away," I said.

"Are you joking? I've run away more times than I can count!"

She didn't say it like she was boasting; just matter of fact.

"Is that why you're down here?" said Honey.

"Nah! I'm down here cos my mum said she'd had enough of me. Said she couldn't cope any more. But when I was younger I used to go off all the time."

Honey and I were both staring at her, like mesmerised.

"Where did you go?" I said.

"Anywhere took my fancy. First time I ended up round my nan's. She used to live in Walmley. Like just a bus ride away?"

I nodded. I knew Walmley.

"They got in a bit of a flap about that, cos I was only eight. They thought I'd been abducted."

"Did they go to the police?"

"Yeah, but then my nan rang and said I was with her."

"So where d'you go the second time?"

"Don't think I went anywhere, really. Just had a bit of a walkabout and came back. I was only away for, like, a few hours."

Honey said, "But what did you do it for?"

"I dunno." Darcy shrugged. "Got the hump about something. One of my mum's blokes, prob'ly. Jack. He was a right so and so! Used to throw his weight around, think he could tell me what to do. *Me!* Like he was my dad, or something. In the end I said I wasn't standing for it any more and I just got out."

Eagerly I said, "Like me! That's what I did."

"You have to. You can't let them get away with it."

"So where did you go that time?" said Honey.

Darcy gave one of her cackles. "Went up north with a mate. Went to Newcastle and stayed with this guy we knew. We were there nearly a week before they got on to us. That was in Year 7, that was."

I said, "I don't remember you going off!"

"Well, I did," said Darcy.

"They never told us."

"No, well, they wouldn't, would they? Might have got all the rest of you at it!"

I hadn't specially been friends with Darcy in Year 7; it wasn't till Year 8 that we'd started to hang out. We'd quite often bunked off school together, but only the odd day, nothing major – though Dad, needless to say, had gone ballistic when he found out. That had been another of our big rows. He'd have shot through the roof if I'd ever tried a stunt like running off to Newcastle.

Or maybe he wouldn't. Maybe he'd have been only too glad to get rid of me.

"You still gotta be careful," said Darcy. "Just cos you're not on the telly doesn't mean they're not looking for you."

"Why do other people get on the telly and not us?" said Honey.

"Like I told you," said Darcy, "I didn't."

"No, well…" Honey didn't actually say it, but I knew what she was thinking. It was what I was thinking myself. Darcy had been running away and bunking off school and getting into trouble ever since she was little; it was only what people expected of her. But me and Honey weren't like that! Honey had never been in trouble her whole life, and even I had never done anything worse than a bit of mini shoplifting. Nothing big time! It wasn't like I was a hardened criminal.

"See, it'd be different," said Darcy, "if you were just little kids. A couple of ten year olds, they'd really pull out all the stops."

I swallowed. "So you don't think they'll ever have my mum and dad on?"

"What, with all the guff about *Come home, all is forgiven?*" Darcy flung out her arms. "*My baby, my baby, we just want you back!*"

"Yeah, well." I tried to match my tone to hers. "Something like that."

"What about my mum?" said Honey.

"Forget about your mum," said Darcy. "She's a lost cause, what I hear. And your dad!" She turned, to look at me. "Can't see him shedding any tears."

Neither could I; not if I were honest. Dad wasn't the sort of person to break down and cry. Mum and Dad on the television, pleading for me to come home. But what was I going to do if they didn't? I hadn't made any plans! Always, at the back of my mind, I'd imagined Mum weeping on the screen, Dad with his arm around her. *We just want her back!*

It wasn't going to happen; I could see that, now. Running away had been the easy part. It was what to do next that was the problem.

Darcy said, "Live for today, that's my motto."

I thought it had been mine, too; but you couldn't just ignore tomorrow!

"Let's do something," said Darcy. She said that now we didn't look like our old selves any more it would be safe to go out. "I'll take you up the West End. Show you the shops. C'mon!"

I was quite eager, because the one time I'd come to London, with Mum and Dad, we hadn't gone anywhere near the West End. Mum had said it was a tourist trap, Dad said it was a temple to mammon, whatever that was. I think he meant people spending their money and having a good time. We'd gone to the British Museum, instead. Which I did enjoy, as it has some extremely interesting things in it, but I would have liked to walk up Oxford Street and see all the big stores.

Darcy promised that that was what we would do. Honey said, "What about the baby?"

"Bring her with us," said Darcy.

"To *Oxford* Street?"

"Why not? What d'you think's gonna happen to her?"

"She might get snatched," said Honey.

Darcy looked at me and rolled her eyes. I rolled mine back at her. Honey was as bad as my dad! I told her not to be so daft, but there was no budging her. She said she'd heard about that part of London.

"Oxford Street, Soho... the West End!"

She'd seen a programme about it on the television. It was full of muggers and drug dealers.

"It's not safe to take a baby to a place like that!"

In the end we said OK, we'd

leave her at home with the baby while we went to Oxford Street to look at the shops and get mugged.

"You shouldn't joke about it," said Honey. "It happens all the time! People are murdered in broad daylight, just for their mobile phones."

"Yeah, well, just don't worry about it," said Darcy. "Nobody ain't gonna mug *me*! I dunno why you ever bothered bringing that girl with you," she grumbled, as we closed the front door behind us. "She's definitely one slice short of a sandwich."

"She's good with the baby," I pleaded.

"Yeah, I s'ppose there is that," agreed Darcy. "Saves us having to cart it around."

I couldn't help wondering whether Darcy's sister had actually wanted a baby, or if it were just "one of those things". I thought probably it was just one of those things, and for a moment I felt sorry for it and could understand why Honey was so protective. Why she kept saying, "Poor little thing!"

I didn't like to ask Darcy in case it seemed like I was prying or being critical. After all, it wasn't really any business of mine.

I enjoyed seeing all the shops and the people in Oxford Street, though not quite as much as I thought I would. I'm not sure why. Maybe it was Honey, putting ideas into my head; or maybe it was the nagging thought, which was there all the time, that not even Mum seemed to care if I'd run away. I hadn't done it to make her unhappy, and I didn't actually *want* her to be unhappy, but I did want her to care!

Darcy told me to stop brooding. She said, "At least your mum never threw you out."

"Yours didn't throw you out," I said. "She just couldn't cope."

"Comes to the same thing."

"Not really," I said. "You were pretty mean to her."

"That's right, take her side," said Darcy. "What do you know about any of it?"

I muttered, "Only what I saw."

"Yeah? And what was that?"

"You treated her like she was just stupid." A bit like Honey's mum had treated Honey. I don't know what made me bold enough to say it; I'd never stood up to Darcy before. This angry black look came over her face. She snapped, "Maybe she was just stupid!"

"She was your *mum*," I said.

"So? That doesn't mean she can't be stupid, does it? All those jerks she used to bring home! I could have told her they were just out for what they could get."

"I always felt sorry for your mum," I said.

"Yeah, well, you're just a soft touch," said Darcy.

I resented that. I wasn't a soft touch! I prided myself on being quite tough and street smart. Darcy sneered and said who did I think I was kidding? Then she started on again about Honey; about me "lugging her along like a bit of extra baggage." She said she was useless.

"A total no-hoper!"

I said, "At least Honey doesn't leave poor little innocent babies to starve while she goes out enjoying herself!"

That did it. We had this terrible shouting match, standing on the edge of the kerb. People kept swerving to avoid us, cars and cabs swished past, almost within touching distance, and we just stood there, yelling at each other.

When it was all over, when neither of us could think of anything else to yell, I thought that Darcy would most probably flounce off and leave me. I wasn't going to flounce off and leave *her*, cos by now we weren't in Oxford Street any more and I wasn't too sure how to get back to the tube station. But I wasn't going to apologise, either! I waited for one of us to say something. It was Darcy who spoke first.

"Well, we got that lot off our chests," she said. "Let's go back and have a gander in Gap."

It was so extraordinary! It was like we'd never stood there on the kerb yelling at each other. By the time we'd mooched all round Gap, and several other stores, trying on various articles of clothing, we were the best of mates again. I thought it was good that we could say all those things and not bear grudges. It wasn't till we were on the tube on the way home that Darcy showed me what she had brought with her from the last shop we'd been in.

"Da-dum!"

With a flourish, she whipped something out from under her T-shirt. I recognised it at once as a Lycra top we'd both fancied.

I said, "How did you *do* that?"

"I got the knack," said Darcy. She grinned. "Want me to teach you?"

"No!" I shook my head. I didn't care what she thought of me, I wasn't getting into that again.

"Call yourself street smart?" jeered Darcy. "You ain't got what it takes, girl. You'll never be a survivor!"

"I've survived so far," I said; but I had this sinking feeling that she might be right.

We got back to find Honey cosily chatting in the sitting room to the big slob from Soup 'n Sarnies. *Joe.* He jumped up when he saw me and Darcy, like he knew he had no right to be there. Honey ought never to have let him in! For one thing (as I somewhat crossly said to her, when he'd gone) this was Darcy's place, not hers. You don't go inviting total strangers into other people's houses. Flats. Whatever. For another thing, we were supposed to be keeping a low profile.

I read her a long lecture about it, but for once she seemed unrepentant. I mean, normally she took notice of what I said. Normally she would have been ashamed

149

of herself. Today she just looked me in the eye and said
boldly that she couldn't see she'd done anything wrong.

"He just came to check how I was. He brought me
these lovely flowers. Look!" She nodded proudly at a
bunch of brightly-coloured something or
others (I'm not very good at flowers)
which she'd stuck into a jug. "I
couldn't be rude to him!"

"You didn't have to let him in,"
I said.

"But he came round specially!"

"Yeah, and that happens to be a
measuring jug." Darcy snatched at it,
angrily. "You trying to poison us?"

"I'm sorry," said Honey. She didn't actually sound
sorry; she sounded more like defiant. "I couldn't find a
proper vase."

"That's probably cos we haven't got one."

"Well, don't just pull them out, you'll kill them!"
Honey took the jug back, cradling it protectively the
way she'd cradled the baby. "Find something else I can
put them in."

Darcy stared, like she couldn't believe what she was
hearing. I couldn't, either. Nobody, but nobody, gave
orders to Darcy! Specially not a no-hoper like Honey.

"*Please*," said Honey.

"Oh, just leave them where they are!" Darcy flung herself into an arm chair, hooking her legs over the side. "What's it matter if we all go down with the green galloping gunge?"

I wasn't bothered so much about gunge. I was more concerned with what Honey might have told fat slob Joe. I said, "What did he mean, when he left?"

He'd looked at me and shaken his head and said, "You didn't have to go and do that to her."

"What did he mean? I didn't have to go and do that to you?"

Honey blushed. "He meant my hair. He doesn't like it like this, and neither do I!"

"I told you," said Darcy. "It'll grow out."

I said, "Yeah, and what's it to do with him, anyway?"

"He said you shouldn't have done it!"

He had some nerve.

"I did explain to him," said Honey.

"Explain?" Alarm bells had started to clang, loudly, inside my head. "Explain what, exactly?"

"Why you had to do it."

"You *told* him?"

Honey munched, on her lip.

"You did," I said, "didn't you? You went and told him! You *idiot*!"

"It didn't make any difference," muttered Honey. "He'd already guessed."

"Like he's some kind of genius?" Darcy swung her feet back to the floor. "He's got a brain the size of a pea!"

Accusingly I said that if Joe had guessed it must have been because of something Honey had said when she'd been on her own with him in the caff.

"I knew I shouldn't have left you! I knew you couldn't be trusted. Now he'll go straight to the police!"

"He won't," said Honey. "I made him promise. I told him that your dad used to hit you and that's why you had to run away, and why you couldn't be sent back." She announced it with an air of triumph. "I said that if you went back he'd bash you to a pulp."

I stared at her, in outrage. How dare she tell such wicked lies about my dad? He might be a bully, and a self-righteous pain, but he'd never laid so much as a finger on me. Not once, in all the humungous great rows we'd had.

Angrily, I said, "Did you tell him that your mum was a raging alcoholic?"

Honey's cheeks turned slowly scarlet.

"Well," I said, "did you?"

With dignity, Honey said, "I didn't have to invent excuses why I couldn't go back. I'm sixteen. I can do what I like!"

With that, she marched from the room, taking her flowers with her.

"I'm sixteen," squeaked Darcy. "I can do what I like!"

"She is," I said. "She is sixteen."

"Yeah, sixteen going on six! I told you you shouldn't have brought her."

I thought to myself that if I hadn't had Honey to keep me company, I probably wouldn't have been brave enough to run away. But I wasn't going to admit that to Darcy, so I just grunted and went, "Maybe."

"No maybe," said Darcy. "I bet he's on the phone right now. Hey, did your dad really used to bash you?"

I said, "No, he didn't! She had no right to say that."

"But her mum is an alky?"

I frowned. "I don't know; p'raps she just drinks a lot. But my dad's never bashed anyone, ever!"

I spent the rest of the afternoon and most of the evening waiting for a knock at the door. Well, or more likely a *hammering* at the door. Or even the sound of splintering wood and the door crashing open as the whole place flooded with armed men. When I told Darcy, she said I was mad.

"They're not gonna send armed cops just for a couple of teenage girls! Who d'you think you are? Al-Qaeda, or something?"

"They're not going to come anyway," said Honey. "I told you… I made him *promise*. He gave me his word."

I muttered, "What makes you think he's going to keep it?"

"He will," said Honey.

"But suppose he doesn't?" I hadn't run away just to be picked up by the police. That wasn't how I wanted it! I wanted Mum and Dad on the television, pleading with me. I wanted to go home of my own accord, not be taken back in disgrace.

"Just chill," said Darcy. "You can always go and hide in a cupboard."

When it came to bedtime and the door still hadn't been battered down, I began to relax a bit. If Joe had given us away, they'd have been round in a flash.

"I told you it'd be all right," said Honey.

"We're still not on the news!"

Darcy rolled her eyes. "There she goes again! You've got ideas above your station, you have. Think the whole world's gonna come to a standstill just cos you've run away from home?"

"It's probably better if we're not on the news." Honey said it as if it had just struck her. "That way, maybe, nobody'll ever come looking for us."

I said, "Yeah, right."

"We don't *want* them to," said Honey, "do we?"

I said no, I supposed not.

"So why do we want to be on the news?"

"Cos she wants it both ways," said Darcy. "She doesn't wanna be caught, but she wants to feel important. She wants to be a celeb!"

"*Do* you?" said Honey.

I snapped, "No, of course I don't! Just shut up talking about it. I'm going to bed!"

Next morning, I woke up feeling quite miserable; I don't know why. But it was like all sense of purpose had vanished from my life. I'd been so bound up, the last couple of weeks, what with plotting and planning, and laying clues. Then there'd been the excitement of actually taking off, and getting down to London, and finding Darcy. Now, suddenly, it had all gone flat.

I was at a really low point, so that when Darcy made her surprise announcement shortly after breakfast, I just went to pieces. The telephone had rung, and Darcy had gone off to answer it. When she returned she said, "Well, sorry, guys, but that's it! My sister's coming back, you'll have to go."

I said, "G—go? Go where?"

"Not my problem," said Darcy.

"But why? I mean, what—I mean—"

"Look, you can't stay here," said Darcy. "There's not enough room, for one thing, and anyway, who's supposed to pay for all your food?"

"But what are we going to do? We don't know anyone, we don't have anywhere else to go to!"

"Shoulda thought of that before."

"I did think of it before! You told me we could always crash here."

"I said *you* could crash here, and I didn't mean indefinitely. I just meant for a day or two. You've been here a day or two."

"B—b—" My mouth was opening and shutting like a goldfish, without any words coming out. Just bubbles of sound.

"Probably be best," said Darcy, "you just turn tail and go home. *She's* not fit to be out on her own, and what d'you think you're gonna do?"

"Find a job," said Honey.

"A job? You must be joking!"

"I'm sixteen," said Honey. "I can work."

"Yeah? Doing what?"

"Anything! I'll earn enough for both of us."

I finally managed to stop blowing air bubbles and say something. "We'll both find jobs! There must be some way of making money."

"Not anything you'd wanna know about," said Darcy. "You wouldn't last five minutes! Just go home," she said, "and play with your Barbie doll."

She wanted us out by two o'clock. She said her sister was coming back that afternoon and we had to be gone before she arrived.

"She'll do her nut if she thinks the police are gonna turn up!"

"The police aren't going to turn up," whispered Honey, as Darcy whisked herself off down the hall. "Why is she doing this?"

I shook my head, helplessly.

"It's cos of me, isn't it? If it was just you, she'd let you stay!"

"She wouldn't, you heard what she said. She doesn't want either of us."

"So what are we going to do?"

"I don't know!" I heard the words come wailing out of me. As a rule I am a very positive sort of person; I can sum things up and make decisions quite quickly. But my brain seemed to have gone into a state of shock.

Honey sat there, waiting. I felt this terrible sense of responsibility. Honey trusted me! I was the one who'd encouraged her to run away, I was the one who'd planned it all, it was up to me to come up with a solution – and I couldn't. I just felt completely useless. I also felt a bit scared.

"Jade?" said Honey. "What are we going to do?"

In defeated tones I said, "I guess we'll just have to go home."

"No!" Honey thumped with her fist on the table. "I'm not going back! Not ever!"

"But—"

"No! I'm not!"

"But what else can we do? We can't live on the streets!"

"I know what we'll do," said Honey. "We'll go and ask Joe."

eight

I really couldn't see what good it was going to do, asking Joe, but Honey seemed set on it and I didn't feel strong enough to fight her. We shoved all our stuff into our rucksacks and told Darcy that we were off.

"It's for the best," she said. "Let's face it… you'd have had to go back sooner or later."

"We're not going back," said Honey. "We're—"

"Don't tell me!" Darcy clapped her hands to her ears. "I don't wanna know! It's safer that way. Case they come looking for you… I can say I've got no idea where you are."

"Oh. All right! That's a good idea." Honey slung her rucksack over her shoulder and opened the door. I trailed dismally after her.

"See ya!" said Darcy.

I said, "Yeah, see ya." But I didn't honestly think that I'd ever want to. Partly because she'd chucked us out, but also because I wasn't terribly sure that I really liked her any more. She'd changed, since coming to London. In the old days she'd been fun, but now she seemed quite cold and hard. Or maybe she'd always been like that and I'd just never seen it.

Honey obviously felt that I needed cheering up. In this bright, breezy voice, like she was talking to a child, she said, "Joe will think what to do!" I made a hrrumphing sound. I had absolutely *no* faith in Joe. As far as I was concerned, he was nothing but a podgy slob with the IQ of a mollusc.

"It's the baby I feel sorry for," said Honey. "Poor little thing!"

I felt like snarling, "Never mind the baby! What about us?"

"The baby'll be all right," I said, instead. "It's going to have its mother back."

"Yes, but I don't think she looks after it properly. I don't think she loves her enough. I wish we could have brought her with us!"

"Well, we couldn't," I said.
"You can't go round kidnapping
babies."

Soup 'n Sarnies was full of
people eating their lunch.

An old lady was behind the counter; Honey told me
she was Joe's nan. Unlike Joe, she was very small and
frail-looking. She shot us an inquiring glance, out of
beady eyes, then Joe himself came lumbering over,
wiping his hands on a tea towel, with this big soppy grin
on his face.

He sat us down at a table in a dark corner.

"Get you some food," he said. "Ham sarnies?"

I could really have gone for a ham sarnie, but Honey
had to go and tell him I was a vegetarian so he brought

me a cheese and tomato bap, instead. There is no denying that having principles involves *a great deal of sacrifice*, but I forced myself to smile and be polite and tried not to be too aware of Honey, happily munching at my side.

Joe pulled up a chair and asked us how things were going.

"We've had to leave," said Honey. "We've been thrown out."

"That's not good," said Joe.

"No, it's not," said Honey. "We don't know where to go. We can't go back home!"

Joe frowned. He turned, solemnly, towards me. "You ought to go to the police," he said.

"You can't let your stepdad bash you and get away with it."

I glowered at Honey. She was responsible for this! Blackening my dad's name.

"'Tisn't right," said Joe. "He's the one ought to leave home, not you."

Honey wriggled, uncomfortably, on her chair. I noticed that she was deliberately avoiding looking at me.

"Dangerous, a young girl like you on her own."

"She's not as young as all that," said Honey. "It's her

birthday next week. Isn't it?" She nudged at me with her foot under the table. "She's going to be sixteen."

Joe turned, somewhat doubtfully, to look at me.

"She can do what she likes, then," said Honey.

"All the same..." Joe shook his head. "You ought to be back with your mum!"

"Oh, her mum doesn't want her," said Honey. "She wouldn't have her back."

What??? I scraped my chair away from the table, with a great clanging and clatter.

"I'm going to the loo," I said.

As I came out of the loo I almost bumped into Joe, carrying mugs of coffee to one of the tables. He nodded gravely at me and said, "It's all right. All taken care of!"

"What did he mean?" I said to Honey. "All taken care of?"

"It's all taken care of! I told you Joe would help us. He said if you really didn't want to go home we can stay here, with him and his nan."

"Stay *here*? In this place?"

"Why not?"

"Cos it's disgusting!" The loo was even more primitive than the ones at school. A horrible little cell, so narrow you could hardly turn round, with great spidery cobwebs hanging in the corners. "It's a dump!"

"That is a really rude thing to say," said Honey.

"It's the truth," I said. "It's a dump!"

"So where else are we going to go?"

I thought glumly that we really didn't any alternative; we would have to go back whether we liked it or not. Darcy was right: I wasn't a survivor. I'd thought I was street smart, but I was beginning to feel more and more helpless and frightened.

"I'm not going back," said Honey. "I'm not ever going back!"

Why wasn't Honey feeling helpless and frightened? Always, before, she'd followed my lead; now suddenly she was the one making all the arrangements and coming to decisions.

"Your mum must be missing you," I said.

Honey hooked her hair over her ears. "She won't be missing me. She doesn't like me."

It was somehow quite chilling, to hear Honey say that.

"She's always been ashamed of me. She thinks I'm stupid."

"You're not stupid!"

"I am a bit," said Honey.

"You're not! Think how you looked after the baby."

"That's different. There's nothing to just looking after a baby."

I told her that I begged to differ. I couldn't have done it! I wouldn't even have known where to begin.

"I bet if you wanted," I said, "you could train to be a nursery nurse, or something. Working with babies! You'd like that."

"Not if it means going back," said Honey. Then she put it to me, straight. "You were the one that told me I had to leave."

"Yes, because your mum was really mean to you, but maybe while you've been away she's, like… thought about things. Like maybe my dad has. So if we go back, it'll be different. You know?"

"I'm not going back," said Honey. "I don't want to go back! If I'm not there, my mum can get on with her life. *She doesn't want me!*"

I muttered that she didn't actually know that; not for certain.

"I do know it," said Honey. "She's told me, lots of times."

"Only when she's drunk! People don't always say

what they mean when they're drunk."

"That's exactly when they say what they mean. *You* can go back," said Honey. "I'm staying here. Joe says I can have his room – we can have his room. If you stay. He'll sleep downstairs. He says it would be really helpful if we could take over some of the work from his nan, cos she's got these bad knees? Like arthritis? He says he couldn't afford to pay us much, but we'd have free food and somewhere to sleep." Honey looked at me, earnestly. "It's better than being on the streets!"

I grunted.

"Anyway, I told him we were grateful," said Honey.

"You told him we'd do it?"

"Yes! I did. Well, I told him I would."

I heaved a sigh. I desperately didn't want to, but if we weren't going to go home I honestly couldn't think what else we could do. "What about the old lady?" I said. "What's he going to tell her?"

"He'll think of something."

"Like what?"

"Something."

"God, this is so exciting," I said. "I can't wait! The big brain swings into action."

I felt ashamed the minute I'd said it; it was mean of me. I didn't have any cause to be snotty with Honey, when all she was doing was trying to solve our problems for us. It was just that nothing was working out the way I'd imagined. Staying with a fat slob and his ancient old gran in a tatty caff? It wasn't in the least bit romantic. If anything, it was *sordid*. But if Honey wasn't going to give in and creep back with her tail between her legs, then neither was I.

"He doesn't have to let us stay," said Honey. "I think it's really nice of him."

"He's only doing it because he fancies you," I said.

She blushed at that, but she didn't deny it. I thought, heavens! Don't say she's *flattered*? Plenty of far better-looking boys than old slob-like Joe had fancied her. What on earth did she see in him?

Honey, as if reading my thoughts, said, "I bet *he* wouldn't leave poor little babies to starve."

"No," I said, "but he'll probably want us to work our fingers to the bone. Cheap labour, that's all we'll be. Nothing comes for free... not in this life!"

The next day, we started work. I'd never had a job before; the most I'd ever done was help Mum and Dad in the shop occasionally, during school holidays. I'd quite enjoyed stacking shelves and putting prices on things. Dad didn't like me taking money, but sometimes when he wasn't there Mum used to let me, and that had always made me feel pleasantly important.

I didn't feel in the *least* bit important working for Joe and his nan. His nan said I wasn't old enough to serve people, so mostly what I got stuck with was doing the washing up. Mounds and mounds of washing up, cos they didn't have a dishwasher. *Or* rubber gloves, which meant my hands had to go plunging into horrible greasy water. The water wouldn't have been greasy if they'd let me use the proper amount of washing-up liquid, but the old lady  got well fussed the first time I did it and screeched that I'd bankrupt them if I carried on like that. So then she made me measure it out in teaspoons, and hung around behind the counter spying on me to make sure I didn't overdose on Fairy Liquid.

When I wasn't washing up I was sweeping the floor, or mopping the tables, or cleaning the beastly horrible coffee machine. I hated that coffee machine! It was always going wrong and spewing its contents over everything. Sometimes it spat hot coffee grounds at me; other times it blew off great clouds of steam.

Honey was luckier: *she* got to play waitress. She also got to make sandwiches and do a bit of cooking. I didn't mind not being allowed to cook as it was mostly fried stuff, like eggs-bacon-sausages, and you got all covered in dobs of grease and smelled of cooking fat; but making sandwiches would have been a change from everlastingly washing up. Joe did let me have a go at it, right at the beginning. I made a great pile ready to be delivered to a nearby office... ham, cheese, beef, salami. I was quite proud of them! But then the old lady came tottering in to take a look, and let out this

indignant squawk. It seemed I'd used way too much of everything. *Again.* Too much ham, too much cheese, even too much marge, for goodness' sake. That was when she said I'd better stick to cleaning duties.

I had the feeling that Joe's nan wasn't too keen on me being there. She was OK with Honey, but she always seemed a bit suspicious of me, like she didn't really believe that I was going to be sixteen in a few days' time.

Honey said, "I had to tell them that! If they knew you were only fourteen they'd call the police."

"Yeah, like if they knew my mum really wanted me back... telling them she didn't! How could you do that?"

"I was only trying to help," said Honey. "I found us a job!"

"So how long do you think you're going to go on doing this *job*?" I said.

"We can do it as long as we like! We can do it till you're really sixteen, and then—"

"What?"

"Get other jobs! If we want to."

Honey seemed in her element, waiting tables, doing the cooking. She was all busy and bustling and full of a happy sense of her own importance. Joe was pleased cos the customers liked her. She smiled at them and talked to them and laughed at their jokes. We'd only been there a couple of days and she seemed to know

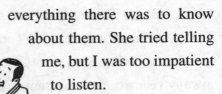

everything there was to know about them. She tried telling me, but I was too impatient to listen.

"How come you don't get bored?" I said. "I'd be bored out of my skull!"

"The customers aren't *boring*," said Honey. She sounded quite shocked. "It's nice, hearing all about their families and stuff."

I said, "Whatever turns you on."

"Don't you like it here?" said Honey.

"What's to like?"

"I like it!"

I didn't know how she could, but she and Joe got on like a house on fire. Honey had discovered that Joe was a fan of the Beany Boys, and they played their CDs till I thought that I'd scream. The Beany Boys are just so naff it's unbelievable. I mean, that anyone would ever have bothered recording them in the first place! I sat and sulked, and worried about the future. I just couldn't imagine still being here, mopping floors and scrubbing tables, in two years' time. But where else could I go? What else could I do?

Honey insisted that once I was sixteen I'd be able to do anything I wanted. I said, "Like go to uni? I don't think so!"

Honey munched on her lip; she didn't have an answer to that. Joe said, "You want to go to uni, you got to study. You want to study, you got to go back to school."

I felt like hitting him. Stupid slob-like thing! How could I go back to school with the police out searching for me?

"Soon as you're sixteen," said Joe. "Do anything you like, when you're sixteen."

Later, crammed next to Honey in Joe's single bed, I grumbled that "It'll be way too late by the time I'm sixteen."

Honey said, "Joe doesn't know that."

Joe might not, but I did. "I'm going to have to waste two whole years!"

I'd never seriously considered going to uni before. I'd always thought vaguely that I might – but then again, I might not. Now, suddenly, it had become a burning ambition. My one aim in life. *I had to get to uni!* I didn't want to end up scrubbing tables. I didn't even want to end up waiting tables. I wanted a proper career!

I said this to Honey. Trying to be helpful, she suggested that maybe I could enrol at one of the local schools.

"Cos maybe," she said, "the police aren't looking for us at all. Maybe they've given up."

"No!" I almost shouted it. "They can't have done!"

Not already! Mum would never let them give up so quickly. She'd be calling them every day, nagging at them. Pleading with them. *Find my daughter...* I knew she would!

"You don't *want* them to come looking?" said Honey.

I wanted them to *be* looking; I didn't want them to actually find me. I wanted to go back of my own accord. I wanted Mum and Dad to tell me they still loved me!

One morning, when I was on my own, scrubbing the stupid counter, the door clanged open and Darcy came breezing in.

"Thought it was you! You taken up residence?"

I said, "Just until something better turns up."

"Wouldn't take much to be better than this lot." She gave one of her cackles. I found it quite annoying.

"Why aren't you at school?" I said.

"Didn't feel like it. Only go when I'm in the mood. Which isn't that often!" She cackled again, and I felt a strong desire to slap her with my wet dishcloth.

"I'm going up west, meet some mates. Wanna come?"

Primly I said, "No, thank you. I've got work to do."

"Oh, well, suit yourself." She flapped a hand. "See ya!"

With that, she breezed back out. I watched as she walked up the road, in the direction of the Underground. I didn't want to end up like Darcy, I thought. I couldn't imagine how I'd ever been friends with her. She was a stupid, stupid person!

Joe came out through the bead curtain which separated the caff from the private living space.

"Who's that, then?" he said. "Your mate from the flats?" He wandered across to the window and squinted out at Darcy's disappearing figure. "She's a bad 'un, that one."

A week ago, if he'd dared say that, I'd have leaped to Darcy's defence; now I thought that he was probably right. Which meant that Dad had been right, too, when he'd wanted to send her packing.

"You shouldn't be friends with the likes of her," said Joe. "You got more going for you than that."

Maybe I had; but all I was doing was sweeping floors and cleaning counters.

"Back to school," said Joe. "That's your best bet."

Although he stayed open till seven o'clock every night, Joe had said that five was to be our "knocking-off time". Honey would willingly have worked right through, but Joe wouldn't let her.

"Can't afford to pay you overtime."

Honey said, "*Over*time? I don't want *over*time."

She was so naïve! Even I knew that you had to get paid extra for working longer hours.

"I just want to help," she said. "I don't want to be *paid*."

176

But Joe shook his head. "Can't have that," he said. "Against union rules."

Honey giggled. "We don't belong to a union!"

I thought to myself that if we did we'd be earning a whole lot more than Joe was giving us. I bet he was making a small fortune! He was just using me and Honey; we were nothing but a convenience.

"Don't you worry about no unions," said Joe. "I'll see you all right! You go off, now, and relax."

"But you'll be on your own!"

That was Honey, needless to say. Not me! Joe told her he could manage. He said his nan would help out for the last couple of hours.

"You go and sit down and watch a bit of telly. I reckon you've deserved it."

So did I! My legs were aching from standing up all day, and my hands were red raw from all the beastly washing up. The first few nights, I just flopped down in an armchair and went straight to sleep. I had never been so exhausted in my life. Honey, on the other hand, said she didn't feel in the least bit tired.

"It was such fun! I really really enjoy working!"

The morning Darcy came breezing in was our sixth day there. For some reason, her visit really depressed me. That evening, I was overcome by a great sense of despair. An endless future of greasy washing up seemed to loom before me. I curled into my armchair with my knees hugged against my chest and drifted into a foggy kind of sleep. I could dimly hear the sound of the television, but not anything that was being said. It was like I was at the bottom of a deep pit; and way up high, out of sight, out of reach, the world was carrying on without me.

Suddenly, I was jerked into wakefulness by Honey poking at me.

"Jade! Hey!"

"What?" I sprang up, in alarm. Honey pointed urgently at the television.

"Look!"

My mouth gagged open; I actually felt it go. There, on the screen, were pictures of me and Honey. My horrible old school photo.

"They're looking for us!" cried Honey. "They're—"

"Sh!" I wanted to hear what was being said.

"Concern is growing for the safety of two teenage girls who went missing from the Birmingham area over a week ago. Honey de Vito, aged sixteen, and her friend

Jade Rutherford, fourteen, were initially believed to have taken the train to Glasgow to meet up with their boyfriends. It is now thought more likely, however, that they are somewhere in London. Th—"

"How did they find out?" wailed Honey. "How d—"

"*Sh!*"

Jade's parents today issued the following appeal: "Please, Jade, wherever you are, please, please get in touch with us!"

It was Mum. Mum, on the television, just as I'd imagined her! And Dad, as well, standing there with his arm round her.

"Why have th—"

"*Quiet!*"

179

Dad was saying something. I snatched at the remote and bumped up the volume.

"*Just come home to us, Jade. That's all we ask. Nobody's going to be cross with you... we just need to have you back.*"

He wasn't pleading, cos Dad wouldn't. But he wanted me back!

"I thought Darcy said they wouldn't bother," wailed Honey.

"Well, that's it," I said. "They have. That's our cover blown! They'll find us now, for sure."

"I'm not going back," said Honey.

"We don't have any choice!"

"I do, I'm sixteen. I'm not going!"

"They'll find you."

"I don't care! They can't force me. You go. I'm staying!"

"Honey, you can't stay here," I said. "It's horrible!"

A slow flush spread across her face. "I don't think it's horrible. I'm happy! I've never been happy like this before. Running away is the best thing I ever did. I am *not* going back again, not ever!"

I didn't know what to say; I wasn't used to Honey taking a stand against me. I made one last attempt.

"If it's the money you're bothered about—"

"It's not!"

"I mean the money you took from your mum… I'm sure she wouldn't really do you for stealing. She'd just be so relieved to have you back!"

"She wouldn't," said Honey. "She doesn't want me back."

"Of course she does! She's your mum."

"She wasn't on the television. She didn't ask me to get in touch."

"Well – no. But she probably would have, if they'd given her the chance. They probably only had room for two people, and you know my dad, he's really pushy!"

Honey just looked at me. I knew I hadn't convinced her; I hadn't even convinced myself.

"Suppose she had asked you?" I said. "Would you go back then?"

Honey hesitated. Then she said, "No."

"Not even though she's your mum?"

"Mums don't always love their kids," said Honey. "I'll love mine, when I have some. I won't care if they're a bit slow. I'll always love them! But you can't go back when you're not wanted. It's all right!" she said. "You don't have to be sad for me."

How could I help it?

"You go back," said Honey, "cos you don't like it here."

I didn't; I hated it. "I'll tell her you're OK," I said. "I'll tell her you just want to stay where you are."

"You won't give them this address?"

"I won't if they don't ask. But I think they might make me."

"Maybe if you just turned up," said Honey, "like not actually ringing them first... maybe they'd be so pleased to see you they wouldn't bother about me."

Somewhat doubtfully I said that I could always try.

"Please! I really don't want them knowing where I am," said Honey.

I promised that I would do my best. "I'll just turn up on the doorstep."

Once I'd made the decision, I couldn't wait to go. I'd have left right there and then but Joe put his foot down. He said it was too late for me to be travelling all the way up to Birmingham on my own.

"You wait till morning," he said, "then I'll put you on the train myself. Make sure you're safe."

He and Honey both went with me to Euston the next morning. The old lady was left in charge. She looked daggers at me as I came downstairs with my rucksack.

"Always knew you weren't sixteen," she said. "Could have caused my Joe a lot of grief, you could! You get yourself back home and stay there. You're nothing but a troublemaker!"

"I'm sorry," I said. "I didn't mean to be."

"Didn't think, did you? It's all *me me me* with your sort. "

It was Joe who came to my rescue. He said, "Nan, let her be. She's going back, there's no harm done."

At the last minute, as I was about to get on the train, Honey flung her arms round me and whispered, "I'm going to miss you so much!"

"Me, too," I said. "I'm going to miss you! Are you really sure you know what you're doing? It's not too late to change your mind! We could get the next train, go and buy another ticket—"

But she wouldn't. In this really grown-up voice she said, "I do know what I'm doing… honestly!"

I didn't like getting on the train without Honey. Whenever I'd pictured this moment, I'd always pictured us going back together; picking up where we'd left off. Now I was leaving her behind – except that in an odd sort of way, it felt more like Honey was leaving me behind.

"Don't forget," said Joe, "any problems, you go straight to social services. Any signs of violence… you know what I'm talking about."

"If you're talking about my dad," I said, "he's never hit me my whole life!"

*****

Dad kept his word: he didn't get mad at me. There was a moment when I thought he might be going to. It was after I'd walked into the shop and Mum had cried "*Jade!*" and hurled herself at me. We'd hugged and kissed, and Mum had wept, and so had I, a little bit. Well, quite a lot, actually. I was just so glad to be home!

There were customers in the shop, and they were all nodding and smiling, cos everyone knows everyone else's business in Steeple Norton. They'd all have known that me and Honey had run away.

Dad said, "Come into the back," and that was when I thought he was going to get mad at me. His face had that look that it got, with his lips all turned in and his eyes narrowed to slits. But Mum said, "Alec?" in this tone that was like half pleading and half a warning, and I could see that he was struggling.

I said, "Dad, I'm sorry!" and quite suddenly he relaxed. All the crossness went out of him and he did something he'd almost never done before, he put his arms round me and crushed me, really tight, against him.

"Don't ever do that to us again," he said. "These have been the worst ten days of my life!"

Afterwards, we had this long talk, just Dad and me. Dad said that we were both going to have to try a great deal harder from now on.

"Both of us," he said. "Not just you – not just me. Both of us. Right?"

I said, "Right."

He admitted that maybe in the past he'd been a bit

too harsh. I muttered that I'd sometimes done things on purpose to upset him.

Dad said, "Well, I'm a grown-up and you're not a child any more, so we surely ought to be able to work out some way of getting along together. What do you think?"

I thought that this was the first time I could remember Dad ever asking me my opinion. About anything.

"Your mother and I love you very much," he said. "If you ran away on purpose to upset us, you certainly succeeded."

I said again that I was sorry.

"That makes two of us," said Dad. "How about we kiss and make up?"

Dad's not very good at kissing; he's not at all a physical sort of person. It was a bit awkward, and even embarrassing, to be honest. But all the resentment I'd been building up over the years just melted away, cos I knew what an effort it was for him.

Mum told me later that she was so relieved me and Dad had been able to talk at last. She said, "Your going off like that was a total nightmare, but if it brings you and your dad a bit closer then it won't have been all bad."

****

Over a year has passed since I ran away. I've let my hair grow back, much to Mum and Dad's relief. They really *hated* it, all chopped off. Mum said, "I nearly passed out when I saw what you'd done to yourself!" Personally I thought it was pretty cool, and so did most of my mates, but I reckoned I'd caused Mum and Dad enough grief. It's no big deal, having ordinary boring hair, if that's what it takes to make them happy.

Me and Dad still have our spats, I guess we always will. We are very different kinds of people. Sometimes even now Dad will put his foot down, with a great SMASH, so that if I were a poor little butterfly creature I would be utterly crushed and humiliated. As I am not a butterfly, but more of a fighting type, I tend to stick up for myself, and that can lead to trouble. But nothing like as serious as it used to be. It's Kirsty, these days, who sends Dad into apoplexy. She's suddenly become a rebellious teenager, always answering back and trying to have her own way. So much for little Miss Goody Two-Shoes! I just sit there and enjoy it.

I had to tell them where Honey was, of course; I knew that I would. I did point out that she was sixteen.

"If she doesn't want to come back, she doesn't have to. She can do what she likes!"

But apparently that wasn't quite right. She was old enough to leave school – just – but she couldn't stay away from home unless her Mum agreed. She also had to be in what they called "a safe environment". Mum rather anxiously asked me, "*Is* it a safe environment?" I knew she was thinking about me rather than about Honey. I told her that it was. I said, "It's mainly just boring."

"But this boy that was there—"

"Joe," I said. "He's OK. And anyway, there's his nan."

"It hardly sounds ideal," said Mum.

It hadn't been for me; but maybe it was for Honey. Her mum came round to talk to me and I told her about Honey being a waitress, and doing some of the cooking, and how she was enjoying it, and her mum said, "Well, it's probably better for her than living with me. She wasn't ever happy with me." I think my mum was quite shocked; but Mum had never really believed me when I

 said how badly Mrs de Vito used to treat Honey. She always told me that I must be imagining it, or at any rate exaggerating.

In the end, Honey was allowed to stay where she was. We called each other quite a lot during the first few weeks, but as time passed it grew harder and harder to think of things to say.

Honey's life seemed totally bound up in Soup 'n Sarnies. All she wanted to tell me about were the customers, the new menu, the number of sandwiches she'd made. I tried to be interested, but I really wasn't. And I don't think Honey was terribly interested in hearing about my life, either. I'd taken up with Marnie again, I was concentrating on school work, I'd got myself a boyfriend (one that Dad didn't actually do his nut about, even if he didn't altogether approve).

And so Honey and I gradually drifted apart, and I didn't hear anything more until just a few weeks ago when she suddenly turned up, beaming, on the doorstep, with a tiny baby. She and Joe had got married! A year ago I'd have been appalled. Honey and fat slob Joe! In fact he wasn't fat any more, he'd slimmed right down and actually looked quite presentable. Mum said afterwards that he was a "really nice young man. Not a bit like you described him!" The more I thought about it, the more I realised how snobby I'd been. Joe was the best thing that could ever have happened to  Honey. Maybe he wouldn't win Brain of Britain, but he was kind, and gentle, and he loved her. I oughtn't to have sneered.

They'd come on a visit to Honey's mum, to show off the baby. They've called her Star, and she's the sweetest thing! Honey made me hold her, though I didn't really want to. Just for a second I got quite gooey and thought that I wouldn't mind having a baby myself. But not for years and years! I have plans. At the moment they don't extend much beyond getting decent marks in next year's exams. After that – we shall see.

One thing I am *not* going to do is end up working in a greasy spoon. I still have a mark on my arm where the beastly coffee machine spat at me. It's a constant reminder, if ever I'm tempted to listen to music or chat with friends instead of doing my homework. Far more effective than Dad shouting!

Not that he does, any more, it's Kirsten he shouts at now. I reckon she deserves it; I'm sure I was never as tiresome as she was. There are times I even feel a bit sorry for Dad. I can see that I must have tried his patience. Of course we continue to have our differences, I expect we always will, but we are both doing our best to be civilised.

I'm trying to, like, respect his views, even if I don't always agree with them; Dad's trying to accept that I am a person in my own right.

I would say that on the whole we are managing quite well.

He certainly isn't the wicked stepfather I used to make him out to be. He might have these really strange ideas about life and how it should be lived, but he's my dad, and I do still love him in spite of everything.

And I know that he loves me; he's just not comfortable showing his feelings. But, hey, we're all different! It doesn't mean we can't get on together. I am becoming *seriously* tolerant in my old age.